It's

A Mystery

Dorothea Maddox

ROYAL MEDIA
PUBLISHING

Royal Media & Publishing
Jeffersonville, IN 47131
http://www.royalmediaandpublishing.com
royalmediapublishing@gmail.com

Book Cover Design and Layout: Royal Media and Publishing

ISBN: 978-1-955501-33-0

Printed in the United States of America

Table of Contents

A Dying Man's Confession

With tears in his eyes, Lee Valentine lay in a nursing home bed, waiting to die. He looked at Corina Wells as she entered his room.

"Corina, I have a confession," Lee said.

"What is this confession?" Corina asked as she sat beside his bed.

"Over fifty years ago, I was blessed with a beautiful wife. But I did something really bad to have her as my wife."

"What was that?"

Fifty years earlier – Flashback

Darla Meadows visited church with her cousin, Martha Waters. After church, Lee approached Darla, who was sitting on the passenger side of Martha's car and introduced himself.

Reverend Jesse Valentine, Lee's uncle, was delighted to see Lee meet Darla. Jesse looked down at Lee's two small nephews, Robert and Emmitt. "Darla's going to marry your uncle Lee, and she's going to be your future aunt."

Darla looked at Reverend Valentine. "I'm engaged to marry Richard Campton. He's doing drills in Fort Knox this weekend." She looked at Lee and said, "I'm so sorry." Martha then drove away.

"Darla's such a beautiful young lady. It's always been my dream to have a beautiful wife to "show off" to friends and relatives. I want other men to envy me and wish they were me," Lee told Jesse.

"I can arrange that," Jesse told him.

The following Saturday afternoon, Richard and Darla got married at a large church in South Louisville. Lee was the photographer.

"I need you to stand at a distance by yourself and face the buildings across the street. You then look at the camera," he told Richard.

Lee looked down at his camera. "Look at this. I need to refill my camera!"

"Go on and refill your camera," said Richard.

"Thank you."

At that moment, a sniper shot Richard and the bullet hit him in the chest. Richard died instantly.

The preacher immediately ran into the church to call the EMTs. Darla and others tried to perform first aid, but nothing worked. Everyone, including Darla, screamed and cried.

A month after Richard's murder, Reverend Valentine married Darla off to his nephew, Lee.

The Sunday after Lee and Darla's marriage, Reverend Valentine stood at the podium. "Does anybody have a testimony this morning?" he asked his congregation.

"I have a testimony!" Lee stood up. "I needed a wife, and Darla was the only woman I wanted. I now have Darla as my wife. I always wanted a beautiful wife to "show off" to my friends and relatives. I want to be the man all the other men wish they could be."

"Amen, my nephew," responded Reverend Valentine. "God put you here, and you needed a wife. Darla is the only woman you want. If Richard were still alive, then your need of a wife would continue to be unfulfilled."

"That's right!" shouted another congregation member.

Every summer, Lee brought Darla to church events, family events, and company picnics. He used her to "show off" to others.

"I wish I was Lee," said some other men.

"What happened to Darla?" asked Corina.

"Five years after we got married, she died from severe depression. We never had children due to our blood types not agreeing. I guess my using her to "show off" to others caused her to slip into deep depression."

"Do you believe she was depressed because Richard, her first husband, was murdered after they got married? You also treated her like some "toy" for display."

"Like my late Uncle Jesse said, 'God put me here and I needed a wife. Darla was the only woman I wanted. If Richard were still alive, then my need of a wife would go unfulfilled.'"

"Do you know who the sniper was?"

"My late Uncle Jesse was the sniper. He was a sniper in the army. On the day of Richard and Darla's wedding, he was on the rooftop of a building across the street, and he knew when to shoot."

"I have an idea of what you said to let him know when to shoot."

<u>Question</u>: What did Lee say to allow Reverend Valentine know when to shoot?

_____

<u>Answer</u>: Reverend Valentine knew to shoot when Lee shouted, "I need to refill the camera!"

A Shooter in the Park

The Woods family was having their annual family reunion in the park. Jerry Woods drove into the parking lot in a nice, new car. After he got out of his car wearing nice clothes, he pulled a stack of money from his pocket. He then entered the park on foot.

"You look so spiffy," said Grandma Woods to Jerry. "You must have a great paying career."

"Where do you work?" asked Granddad Woods.

"I'm seeing a rich widow, and she loves to spend money on me," Jerry lied.

Suddenly, a man ran into the park and, within shouting distance, said, "You stole my car, my clothes, my money, and my woman!" shouted the man. Later, this man would be known as Anthony Riggs, a man who had a noticeable birthmark on his face.

Anthony pulled out a gun and started to shoot at Jerry. He then shot Jerry in the arm. Some of the witnesses were on the right side of Anthony, the shooter, and others on the left side of him.

Some of them called 911 and others ran to Jerry's aid. Anthony, the shooter, quickly ran out of the park.

The paramedics and the police were in the park within five minutes. The paramedics put Jerry on a stretcher and into the back of the ambulance. The police officers questioned the witnesses. Officer Rodriguez questioned the people who were on the right side of the shooter. Officer Reeves questioned the witnesses on the left side of him. The officers then discussed the stories with each other.

"According to my witnesses, he had a birthmark on his face," said Officer Rodriguez.

"My witnesses didn't say anything about any birthmark on his face," Officer Reeves replied.

Jerry survived the shooting and testified in court against Anthony. Jerry's attorney was Jung Choi. Anthony's attorney was Newt Lynch, the best criminal attorney in town. Anthony was in an orange jumpsuit, in shackles.

Each of the members of the Woods family sat on the witness stand and gave their testimonies. Even Grandma and Granddad Woods testified.

Attorney Lynch stood in front of the twelve jurors and said, "The witnesses' testimonies are inconsistent. According to some of the witnesses, the shooter had a birthmark on his face. According to other witnesses, the shooter had no birthmark on his face. Which one is it?"

The twelve jurors whispered among themselves as Attorney Lynch sat down.

Attorney Choi then stood in front of the twelve jurors. "I know that the witnesses' stories seem inconsistent, but both stories are true." Attorney Choi proceeded with explaining why both stories were true. The jurors looked at each other and nodded in agreement.

The twelve jurors went into the chambers to discuss the issue. They then came out with their verdict and returned to their seats.

"Has the jury reached a verdict?" asked Judge Roy McCoy.

The first juror stood up. "We, the jurors, find Anthony Riggs, the defendant, guilty."

Judge McCoy looked at Anthony. "Mr. Anthony Riggs, the court finds you guilty of attempted murder. You will spend no less than ten years in the city jail."

Judge McCoy looked at the guards. "Guards, please escort the defendant to the jailhouse across the street." He then pounded his gavel. "Court is adjourned."

Anthony began to cry as the guards escorted him out of the courtroom.

Everyone in the Woods family cheered. Everyone in the Riggs family openly wept and wailed.

The guards escorted Anthony out of the courthouse and across the street to the jailhouse.

"That makes no sense," Said Attorney Lynch. "How can both stories be true?" he asked Attorney Choi.

"There's a simple explanation," answered Attorney Choi. He began to explain to Attorney Lynch how both stories can be true.

<u>Question</u>: How can both stories be true?

_____

<u>Answer</u>: Anthony Riggs, the shooter, had a birthmark on the right side of his face, but not on the left side of his face. That's why the witnesses on his right testified that he had a birthmark on his face. But the witnesses on the left side of him testified that he had no birthmarks on him.

A Tale of Three Goldfish

There were three goldfish siblings in the local pet store owned by Joseph Zale and his wife, Jill. This was the only pet store in the small city of Kentville. The first goldfish was named Goldie. Her two brothers were named Treasure and Fort Knox.

Goldie was bought by Pamela Henderson. Pamela kept Goldie in a small fishbowl, and she stayed very small. Pamela was a single lady who live in a small apartment.

Treasure was bought by Randy Meadows and his wife, Wanda. They had a big goldfish pond in their backyard. Like the other goldfish in the pond, Treasure grew to become medium-sized.

Fort Knox was bought by Ron Bivins and his wife, Deloris. They owned land with a large lake on it. Treasure grew to become quite large.

One morning, Pamela decided to bring Goldie to visit each of her brothers. At first, she brought Goldie to visit Treasure at the Meadows' house. Randy and Wanda invited Pamela and Goldie into the backyard.

"Wow!" Pamela said. "Goldie stayed small, but Treasure is medium-sized." She looked at Randy and Wanda. "How can that be?" she asked them.

Randy and Wanda shrugged their shoulders because they weren't sure, either.

"It sounds like an unsolved mystery to me," responded Randy.

Later the same afternoon, Pamela took Goldie to visit her other brother, Fort Knox, at the Bivins' place. Ron and Deloris invited Pamela and Goldie to visit Fort Knox in the lake behind their house. There were "No Fishing" and "No Trespassing" signs near the lake.

Fort Knox jumped out of the water, and Pamela could see that he was large.

"Wow!" said Pamela. "Goldie stayed small. Treasure is medium-sized, and Fort Knox is large. How can that be?"

Ron and Deloris both shrugged their shoulders.

"It sounds like an unsolved mystery to us, too," said Deloris.

One day, Pamela called Wanda. "The cost of everything went up and I can no longer afford to care for Goldie," she told her. "Can Randy and you adopt Goldie?"

"Randy and I would be glad to adopt Goldie," said Wanda. "Just bring her over and we'll add her to the big pond in our backyard."

"Thank you so much." Pamela was relived.

Pamela brought Goldie over to the Meadows' house. Randy released Goldie into their pond.

Six months later, Pamela went to visit Goldie at the Meadows' house.

"Where's Goldie?" Pamela asked Wanda.

"There she is." Wanda pointed to the goldfish with the black spot on top of her head.

"Wow!" said Pamela. "When she was in my fishbowl, she stayed small. Now, she's medium-sized, like her brother, Treasure."

"Joseph Zale is the only person who has the answer," said Wanda. "When the pet store opens, we'll go ask him."

"It sounds like a good idea," replied Pamela.

Pamela and Wanda went to visit Joseph Zale at the pet store.

"There's a perfectly logical explanation," Joseph told the two women.

Joseph then proceeded to explain to both ladies why Goldie stayed small, Treasure grew to become medium-sized, and Fort Knox grew so large. After Pamela allowed the Meadowses to adopt Goldie, she grew to become medium-sized.

Joseph went onto the computer and found a site which was titled, *The life of goldfish: Everything you need to know about goldfish*. Joseph made copies for Pamela and Wanda to read and share with others.

Pamela read the explanation. "Mystery solved," she said.

She then took the papers to Ron and Deloris so they could read them as well.

"Mystery solved," Ron remarked after reading.

Wanda went home with her copy so she and Randy could read about the life of goldfish.

"Mystery solved," Randy and Wanda responded together.

Questions: Why did Goldie stay small, Treasure grew to medium-sized, and Fort Knox grew large? How did Goldie grow to become medium-sized after the Meadows family adopted her?

<u>Answer</u>: Goldfish can only grow according to their environment. If a goldfish is kept in a small fishbowl, then they remain small. If a goldfish is put into a pond, then they grow to become medium-sized. If a goldfish is put into a large body of water, then they become large.

About the Tattoo

Michelle Fawcett, a woman with long, red hair, sunglasses, and a tattoo of a black panther on her left calf, held a gun to Mrs. Venice Bivins.

"I wanted to marry Mr. Berry Bivins! Why did you get to marry a very rich widower with a bad heart?" shouted Michelle before she shot Venice.

Although the incident occurred in a back alley next to a laundromat, several people witnessed the shooting. Michelle remained in jail for two months before she was put on trial.

Michelle showed up in court with short, blonde hair. She also has no tattoo on her left calf.

"All rise!" shouted the bailiff as Judge Troy Brown approached the bench. All the people rose.

"All may be seated," said the bailiff after the judge sat down.

Michelle was in handcuffs and shackles. She was represented by Attorney Newt Lynch.

"Attorney Newt Lynch is the best criminal attorney in the city," Christy Bivins Joyner told her husband, John Joyner.

"Attorney Jung Choi is the second-best attorney in the city. Let's hope he can defeat Attorney Lynch. Venice's murder did trigger a massive heart-attack in your brother, Berry," said John.

"Because of Michelle, we had to bury both Venice and my brother Berry."

Each witness sat on the witness stand and told their version of the story.

"According to everybody who witnessed the shooting, the shooter had long, red hair, and a tattoo of a black panther on her left calf!" Attorney Lynch shouted to the twelve jurors.

Tuffy Carson, the first juror, had a look of skepticism on his face.

Attorney Jung Choi had a look of defeat on his face.

When all the witnesses had been heard, the twelve jurors were called into a back room, and then they closed the door. They were to decide on Michelle's fate.

When Tuffy counted the papers, eleven found the defendant innocent and one decided guilty.

"Who decided guilty when we know Michelle is clearly innocent?" asked Pamela Frank, one of the other jurors.

"I said guilty, and I have my reasons why," Tuffy said.

"Please explain," said Douglas Dorsey, another juror.

"My mother, Cindy, and my two older sisters, Ronda and Danielle, are all hairdressers—" Tuffy started to explain.

"What do the three of them being hairdressers have to do with Michelle being guilty of anything?" Douglas rudely interrupted.

"Some hair colors can be washed in. The hair colors can be washed out after five to ten washes. The unwashed dye can then be cut out," Tuffy explained.

"That makes sense," Pamela agreed. "Michelle was in jail for a month, and she washed her hair almost every day while in jail."

"Also, intern hairdressers come to the ladies' jails once a week to do the inmates' hair for free, to get the practice and experience," Douglas added.

"About the tattoo," Tuffy went on, "I'm a professional tattoo artist."

The other eleven jurors, including Douglas and Pamela, began to listen to Tuffy.

Later, the twelve jurors returned to the courtroom.

"Has the jury reached a verdict?" asked Judge Brown.

Tuffy stood up and read the decision. "In the case of first-degree murder, we, the jury, find Ms. Michelle Fawcett guilty!"

"Ms. Michelle Fawcett, you were found guilty of murder in the first degree. You will serve twenty years to life in the Women's Prison in Pewee Valley, Kentucky," Judge Brown stated.

The bailiff escorted Michelle out of the courtroom. Berry's family and Venice's family all cheered. John and Christy joyfully hugged Attorney Choi.

"Court is adjourned!" shouted Judge Brown as he pounded his gavel.

Attorney Lynch approached Tuffy.

"This makes no sense!" yelled Attorney Lynch. "The murderer had a tattoo of a black panther on her left calf. My client has no tattoo on her body!"

"About the tattoo—" Tuffy started.

"I believe I know what you're about to say!" Attorney Lynch angrily interrupted.

Attorney Lynch approached Attorney Choi and shook his hand.

"You won fair and square. I was defeated," Attorney Lynch told Attorney Choi.

Question: What was it about the tattoo?

_____

Answer: Tuffy was a professional tattoo artist. He knew a temporary tattoo from a permanent one. Michelle wore a temporary tattoo from the "$5 and Less" store. She peeled it off while she was in jail.

Bella and Brenda

Bella entered the *Roadside Diner* wearing an expensive evening gown and snakeskin shoes. She also had an designer purse made from python skin.

"You're dressed mighty fancy for a diner, Bella," Roy Hughes, a local farmer, said.

"This gown is the latest style in Hollywood, California," Bella boasted.

"This isn't Hollywood, California," Pam, Roy's wife, said. "This is a farm town in Kentucky."

"Apparently, you're jealous of me because I'm the widow of an oil tycoon from Texas." Bella had a snooty tone in her voice.

"I'm really happy being married to Roy. We've been together for over forty years. We have four children and twelve grandchildren. I'm happy with who I am and with my life."

"What are you trying to prove?"

"I don't need to be married to some billionaire to be happy."

"I'm the widow of a billionaire, and I have class. I can afford fancy clothes, shoes, and purses. Nobody else in this town can." Bella then walked away and went to sit at a nearby table.

Bella smiled and waved at the single men in the diner. All of the men ignored her.

Floyd McCoy, the most handsome bachelor in town, entered the diner.

"Hello." Bella smiled and waved at Floyd.

Floyd ignored Bella. He started staring at a waitress named Brenda Dunkin.

All of the single men also started to stare at Brenda.

Bella sat at a table, and Ruth Bailey, another waitress, waited on Bella.

"Can I get you some coffee?" Ruth asked Bella.

"I only drink hot tea with lemon." Bella sadly looked at Brenda. "What does Brenda have that I don't? I'm a rich widow. She's the widow whose husband died in a war while in the army."

"Brenda's using her late husband's G.I. Bill to help pay for college. She also works here every Saturday and Sunday to make ends meet." Ruth wrote down what Bella wanted. "I'll bring your tea with lemon."

A few minutes later, Ruth brought Bella's hot tea with lemon and walked away.

"I'm giving you your break. Ralph has fixed your favorite breakfast for you," Ruth said to Brenda as she grabbed some plates of food for other customers.

"Thank you so much." Brenda smiled at Ruth and then looked at the cook, Ralph Lawson. "Thanks so much to you, too, Ralph." She grabbed her breakfast and went to sit down.

"I guess she eats for free because she's the poor widow whose husband died in a war?" Bella asked Floyd, who sat at the next table drinking his coffee. "Why would you want a poor widow who has to work for free meals when you can have a rich widow like me?"

"Women like you have never interested me. I cannot afford to buy you everything you want." Floyd got up, grabbed his coffee, and went to sit with Brenda.

Bella looked disappointed.

"Can I sit here with you?" Floyd asked Brenda.

"Yes, you may." Brenda had a big smile on her face.

"Please tell me about yourself." Floyd sat down and took a sip of his coffee.

"Before Derek, my husband, was deployed to Afghanistan, we lived in many different places. We lived in Germany, England, Italy, and Okinawa, Japan."

"My condolences. My wife, Amy, died from the corona virus three years ago."

"My condolences to you too." Brenda had a sympathetic tone in her voice.

"You have always interested me. Even when you were a little girl who was always traveling around the world with your father." Floyd was impressed.

"I went from being an army brat to becoming an army wife to becoming an army widow who now lives with in her grandparents' house."

"It's all good."

Other single men gathered around Brenda. All of them were equally impressed with the young widow.

Ruth brought Bella another cup of hot tea with lemon.

"Why do the men pay attention to Brenda and ignore me?" Bella asked Ruth again.

Ruth said nothing. She simply looked at Bella's expensive dress, shoes, and purse.

Question: Why were all the men interested in Brenda, and none of them interested in Bella?
_____

<u>Answer</u>: Bella was a woman who only wanted expensive things. None of the men in her town could give her these expensive items.

Born Cursed

During the night, Irene Spicer ran down the street wearing only her bra and panties. An army soldier ran after her with a gun.

"Help me!" Irene shouted. "He's trying to kill me!"

"Give me my wallet back! I only want my wallet back!" shouted the soldier.

"I got four kids to support! I'm not giving you your wallet back!" Irene continued to run.

Some residents shut their windows and blinds. Others turned up their TVs and radios. All the residents ignored Irene's screams.

The soldier grabbed Irene. He dragged her down the street and into her backyard, where he shot her five times.

The next morning, the police surrounded Irene's house. Irene, indeed, had four small children, two boys and two girls. James was five. Joseph was four. Janet was three. And Jane was two. All the children wept over their mother's dead body. James, the oldest, was the angriest.

Detectives Nicole Reeves and Candida Rodriguez collected bullet shells. The coroner put Irene's corpse into the body bag.

Soon after, Reverend Joshua Spicer arrived. "My wife and I will raise James and Joseph. I'm their maternal uncle," he told Detective Reeves. "My wife and I have three daughters and no sons."

Reverend Abraham Bingham arrived shortly afterwards. "My wife, Marsha, and I will raise Janet and Jane. Marsha and I have four boys. She's their maternal aunt and has always wanted daughters."

"Why did Ron King never marry Irene?" Joshua shouted. "He's in the Air Force. He should've married her and raised her children!"

"None of Irene's children belonged to Ron," Abraham explained. "She had her children by four different army soldiers. Why should Ron marry her?"

"Instead of Ron returning with a wedding ring and marriage proposal, he came home with a pregnant wife, Diane!" Joshua was furious. James heard the entire conversation.

"The last time Ron was here, he bought Christmas presents for the children. A man with a gun answered Irene's door and said, 'If you ever again come here, then I'll shoot you! Take your presents and leave!' That was why Ron stopped coming to see Irene," Marsha told them.

"A real man would show up in a bullet-proof vest! Not get involved with another woman, get her pregnant and marry her!" shouted Joshua. "Ron and Diane are having twins, and I curse their first-born child!"

Ron and Diane had their twins in Syracuse, New York. Dironda, a daughter, was their first-born. Theron, a son, was their second-born.

All through school, Theron was always in advanced classes, a straight-A student. Dironda always took special education classes. She passed all her classes with a C or C-.

Theron enlisted in the navy and graduated from the naval academy in San Diego, California at the top of his class. Dironda attended Kentucky State University and took Developmental Educational Studies (DES) classes.

Theron went on to receive Naval Pilot Training and became a pilot. Dironda dropped out of college due to receiving D's and F's in most of her classes.

At thirty, Theron married a beautiful divorcee named Brook. He was deeply loved by his two stepchildren, Laura and Ted. Theron and Brook's wedding was perfect.

Dironda met and married a rich widower named Daniel Bivins. Their wedding was rudely interrupted by Dironda's former college roommate, Michelle Fawcett.

"My sister, Aaliyah, has a baby! They need a place to live. I know that Daniel has a fully furnished townhouse," Michelle told Dironda. Michelle and Aaliyah were with their mother, Priscilla. Aaliyah had her baby, Lana, in her arms.

"Go ask your husband," shouted Priscilla.

Dironda asked Daniel, and Daniel said, "No."

A week after Daniel married Dironda, Daniel was shot by a sniper as he came out to his front porch to get a package.

James Spicer was the judge. He acquitted Michelle Fawcett of murder. He also gave all of Daniel's belongings to Aaliyah.

"Aaliyah Fawcett, you will receive Daniel's fully furnished townhouse. You get his car, and you get all his money," the judge decreed.

James looked at Dironda. "You leave with nothing."

Question: Why was Dironda cursed and not Theron?

<u>Answer</u>: Dironda was the first-born.

What's BR Glass?

"What's BR glass?" asked Frank Evans, James Reeves' maternal grandfather.

"I want to know too," said Dori Evans, James' maternal grandmother.

"These windows will keep you safe," responded James.

"You already got us those doorbell cameras to prevent porch pirates from stealing our packages and keep us safe," Dori told James.

"Grandma, I know some shootings have recently occurred in this neighborhood. That's why I decided to invest in BR windows for you two," James told Dori. "You raised me after my mother was shot and killed when I was five and that bullet came through our kitchen window. To make matters worse, we lived only two houses down from here. Then my father remarried and moved away."

"We're too old to move and start over again," Dori said.

"BR glass sounds fancy," Frank said. "What's it made of?"

"It's made of polycarbonate, acrylic, or glass-clad polycarbonate material. Some BR glass can be made of both polycarbonate and acrylic materials combined," James explained patiently.

"In the old days, when we needed new windows, we just bought plain, old-fashioned, down-to-earth glass windows from a window place," Frank fussed. "Do they still have plain, old-fashioned, down-to-earth glass windows like they had back in my day?"

"Yes, Granddad, they do," answered James, "but I'm paying, and I decided to have BR glass installed. The window installers will produce glass from both polycarbonate and acrylic materials. I also want my wife and children to be safe when they come to visit you two."

"I really enjoy having your wife, Nikki, and your children come to visit us," Dori told him.

"Nikki and our children—Darla, Donald, and Daniel—really enjoy staying here when I have military assignments and can't bring them." James put his arms around Dori.

"To think about it, when Floyd and I die, you and your family will inherit this house."

"At this time, I'm installing BR glass to keep Granddad and you both safe and alive. Nikki, the kids, and I would rather have you two here for as long as God wants you here. We'd rather have both of you than your house." James kissed Dori on the forehead.

"Your granddad and I will not be here forever. That's why we left the house to your family and you," Dori told James.

"I still say that all you need is simple, down-to-earth, good, old-fashioned glass. Not all this fancy glass with names I can't pronounce," Frank said.

"Frank, stop your fussing," said Dori. "This glass might be that kind of sophisticated glass that lasts for fifty years or more. They produce new, more advanced stuff all the time. Like the security system with the doorbell camera."

Frank looked at James. "I have faith in you, Grandson."

"Granddad, I know you've never heard of BR glass for windows. I also know that you never heard of materials such as polycarbonate or acrylic or glass-clad polycarbonate. But trust me, and thank you for having faith in me."

"I heard of a man from this neighborhood named Roderick Cotton who served in the Marines. After the Marines, he became a male model. He used the money from his modeling career to install these fancy windows to low-income residents for free," said Frank.

"I went to high school with Roderick Cotton. He always wanted to accomplish remarkable things and do good things for our community," James said. "Roderick has always wanted to be a male model. One day, he promised God that if he became a male model, then he'd do something good for our community. He carried through with his promise."

"A magazine did a story about him," Dori said.

"I also made a promise to God to do something great for you two," James told his grandparents. "That's why I'm having these "fancy, new age" windows installed for you."

"I still say all we need is windows with simple, old-fashioned glass," Frank said.

"Stop your fussing," Dori told him.

"What is BR glass, anyway?" Frank asked.

James explained about BR glass once again to his grandparents.

Question: What is BR glass?
_____

Answer: BR glass is short for bullet-resistant glass. Some shootings occurred in the past. James had bullet-proof windows installed in his grandparents' house.

Camping Trip Nightmares

Reverend John and Mrs. Daphne Forest sponsored a camping trip for twenty-four preteens the week before Labor Day. They sponsored twelve boys and twelve girls—ages ten to twelve. The Forests also brought along volunteers. Joe "Caveman" Stone was a retired police officer. All the adults were military, peace corps, and police veterans who wanted to do good for others.

"Joe, this is my nephew, Michael Forest. He's my brother's son," John told Joe.

"Is this the man who was trapped in a cave filled with hibernating bears many years ago?" Michael asked John.

"Yes, I am," answered Joe. "As a police officer, I was looking for a criminal who was supposedly hiding in a cave. I stepped on a stick, and it woke up the bears."

"How did you escape?" asked Michael.

"I sang them a song. I sang 'Jesus Loves Me' to them, and they went back to sleep."

"I was told singing to bears can put them to sleep."

"I later found out the criminal was in a different cave."

"It's nice to meet you," Michael said as he walked towards Ted Vessels.

"This is Ted Vessels. He spent some time in Africa when he was in the Marines," John said.

"Nice to meet you," said Ted as he shook Michael's hand. "Did your uncle tell you about the time I escaped from stampeding rhinos?"

"I haven't heard the story yet." Michael laughed. "But I'm sure you plan to share it with me."

"I'll share the story with everyone after dinner," Ted told John and Michael.

"And this is Darwin Lincoln," John told Michael as they approached another man.

"It's nice to meet you," Darwin said as he, too, shook Michael's hand. "Has your uncle ever told you the story of the time I escaped a group of hostile adult chimpanzees in the jungle of Africa when I was in the Peace Corps?"

"I hear that adult chimpanzees can be extremely violent toward humans," said Michael.

John then introduced Michael to all the other volunteers and the twenty-four preteens.

After dinner, each night, a volunteer would share a story with the children. On the first night, Ted shared his story about his "escape" from stampeding rhinos while in Africa. All the children were intrigued by the tale.

Later that night, all the children had nightmares about running from stampeding rhinos. The male volunteers comforted the boys and sang to them until they went back to sleep. The female volunteers did the same with the girls, singing to them until they also went back to sleep.

On the second night, Darwin shared the story of him escaping from a pack of vicious adult chimpanzees. Again, all the children were intrigued.

Later that night, all the children had nightmares about running from vicious chimpanzees. Once again, the male volunteers comforted the boys, singing to them until they went back to sleep. The female volunteers sang to the girls until they fell asleep.

The last night was the Saturday before Labor Day. All the children had nightmares about themselves being trapped in a cave filled with angry bears. The male volunteers comforted the boys and sang to them until they went back to sleep. The female volunteers comforted the girls and sang to them until they went back to sleep.

Sunday morning, John did the sermon. After he closed the Bible, he looked at the volunteers.

"I'm aware of why the children had nightmares about stampeding rhinos on the first night," John said as he looked at Ted.

Ted hung his head in shame.

"I'm also aware of why the children had nightmares about running from vicious chimpanzees." He looked at Darwin.

Darwin hung his head in shame.

"Must we wonder why the children had nightmares about being trapped in a cave filled with bears last night?" John asked.

Question: Why did the children have nightmares about being trapped in a cave filled with angry bears?

Answer: On the last night, Joe shared with the children his experience about being trapped in a cave filled with angry bears. John and Daphne had a "talk" with the volunteers about what kind of stories to share and not share.

Captive Survivor

Chelsea Rouse showed up at the Valdosta, Georgia Police Department with an unusual story. She spoke with Officer Kwang Choi.

"I was held captive in an attic down in Tampa, Florida. I slipped some sleeping pills into the beer bottles of the men who were supposed to guard me, and I escaped," Chelsea frantically told Officer Choi.

"Traffickers normally hold their captives in soundproof basements. How do you know it was an attic?" asked Officer Choi.

"I was kept in an attic and brought out to do the cooking, cleaning, and taking care of their children. It was a husband and a wife. George Jones and Gayle Jones. They had five children. Three boys and two girls."

"I'll take you to the local hospital to be examined by my brother, Jung Choi. I'll also select Shannon Choi, our sister, to be your attorney."

"I have no money. I escaped with only the clothes on my back and shoes on my feet."

"The Georgia Human Trafficking Rescue Task Force raises money for survivors like you. Shannon, Jung, and I all participate in the fund raiser every year."

"You sound like you come from a wonderful family."

"Shannon, Jung, and I are fraternal triplets. Shannon was the first-born. In Southern Georgia, the Choi Family has a reputation for raising money for our state's rescue task force."

Chelsea received new clothes and Shannon was assigned as her pro bono attorney.

With their five children in their minivan, George and Gayle drove up to Georgia looking for Chelsea. The Georgia State Police arrested them immediately. Attorney Newt Lynch, a criminal attorney, was their attorney.

"According to your testimony, the Joneses held you captive in an attic and not a soundproof basement," Attorney Lynch said to Chelsea. "Traffickers hold their captives in soundproof basements—not attics! Attics cannot be made soundproof! Therefore, your testimony makes no sense.

All twelve jurors gave Chelsea skeptical stares. None of them believed she was held captive in an attic instead of a basement. With tears in her eyes, Chelsea got down from the witness stand to sit next to her attorney.

Shannon stood in front of the jurors.

"There's a perfectly logical reason for why Chelsea testified about being held in an attic and not a basement," Shannon began.

All twelve jurors went into the chambers to decide on the verdict. They came out five minutes later.

"Do you have a verdict?" Judge Troy Brown asked the jurors.

The first juror stood up. "We, the jury, find Mr. George Jones and Mrs. Gayle Jones guilty of human trafficking." The first juror then sat down.

"Mr. George Jones, you'll spend twenty years to life in the Georgia State Penitentiary. Mrs. Gayle Jones, you'll spend twenty years to life in the Women's Correctional Center.

The Georgia State Child Protective Services will gain custody of your children." Judge Brown then pounded his gavel and adjourned.

Attorney Lynch leaned toward George and Gayle. "I don't know how you were found guilty," he whispered. "Traffickers hold their captives in soundproof basements—not in attics."

"Guards, take George and Gayle Jones away!" Judge Brown shouted to the guards.

Chelsea excitedly hugged Attorney Choi. Chelsea's parents and three younger brothers were there to congratulate her.

"Praise God!" Rose, Chelsea's mother, shouted. "We prayed for many years for your safe return! Many churches also prayed for you."

Attorney Lynch approached Attorney Choi to shake her hand and congratulate her. "Congratulations. But it makes no sense for Chelsea to be held captive in an attic and not a soundproof basement."

"There's a perfectly logical explanation for Chelsea being held in an attic instead of a basement down in Florida," responded Attorney Choi.

"Ah, now that I think about it, I suddenly remember why it makes sense for the Joneses to hold her captive in an attic and not a basement."

<u>Question</u>: How did they know Chelsea was held captive in an attic and not a soundproof basement?

<u>Answer</u>: Due to much of Florida being swampy, none of the houses in Florida have basements.

Crime Witness

Sandy Beach's birthday was June fifteenth and her sister, Amy Taylor, gave her a gift bag.

"Happy birthday, Sandy. I hope you like it." Amy excitedly handed the gift to Sandy.

Sandy excitedly pulled some perfume out of the gift bag.

"It's perfume called *Strawberry Fields*. I guess being a certified pharmacy technician at the hospital has its benefits."

Sandy sprayed it into the air. "It smells expensive."

"That's why I got it for your birthday. I got it from *The Body Care Shop* in town."

"Are you sure Ms. Ginger Hatchett won't get upset?" Paul Taylor, Amy's husband, interrupted. "Being the granddaughter of a famous movie star from the 1960s and 1970s, the late Jennifer Anderson, Ginger feels like she has certain privileges. She wants to be the only person in Poetstown to wear *Strawberry Fields* perfume."

"After today, I won't buy her any more *Strawberry Fields* perfume. I promise," Amy told Paul.

"Sandy, how can you tell which perfumes are expensive?" Paul asked. "Being that you're..."

"Blind?" Sandy interrupted. "Highly expensive perfume has a stronger smell. The smell enters the room before the person does. Lower costing perfume has a more subtle smell."

"I'll keep that in mind," Amy told Sandy. "Everyone smells Ginger before we see her."

That following September, Sandy and her service dog, Brutus, entered *The Body Care Shop*.

"Welcome to *The Body Care Shop*. If you see anything you want, let me know." Sofia Zane greeted Sandy with a smile.

"Can I please smell some of your perfumes?" Sandy looked towards Sofia.

"Sandy, I'm so sorry." Sofia ran towards her. "I'll let you smell some of our perfumes."

Sofia sprayed *Sandy Beach Coconuts* into the air.

"I like that. It smells nice, and it doesn't smell expensive."

"This is *Sandy Beach Coconuts*. It arrived this morning."

"I'll take it. I'll even take the body wash and lotion."

"Good choice." Sofia bagged the items. "Besides, Ginger wants to be the only person in Poetstown to wear *Strawberry Fields* perfume and use the *Strawberry Fields* items."

"That's fine with me." Sandy handed Sofia a credit card with braille on the front.

That following night, Sandy and Brutus went to *Poetstown Pizza* for dinner. Sandy and Bruno sat outside under the awning. It was dark, but that didn't matter to Sandy.

Mrs. Sadie Perez ran into the back alley beside the restaurant. Ginger chased after Sadie.

"I wanted to marry Mr. Roberto Perez, the founder and CEO of *Spanglish* magazine. Why did you get to marry Roberto?" Ginger shouted before she shot Sadie in the alley.

Ginger ran out of the alley, unaware of Sandy sitting under the awning.

Sandy was appointed to testify on the witness stand.

"This makes no sense!" Attorney Newt Lynch, Ginger's attorney, shouted. "Sandy's blind. She makes an insufficient eyewitness! She cannot give a physical description of the shooter!"

"She can make a suitable witness," Attorney Jung Choi, Roberto's attorney, responded.

"Make that make sense!" Attorney Lynch shouted.

"Proceed with your testimony," Attorney Choi told Sandy.

"I heard Ginger yelling, 'I wanted to marry Roberto Perez, the founder and CEO of *Spanglish* magazine! Why did you get to marry Roberto?' I then heard gunshots."

"What happened after that?" Attorney Choi asked.

"I heard running, and smelled 'Strawberry Fields' perfume."

"There's only one person in town who wears *Strawberry Fields* perfume, and we all know who that is." Attorney Choi turned and looked at Ginger.

Soon, the twelve jurors left the courtroom and went into the chambers to make their decision. Fifteen minutes later, they returned.

"Do you have a verdict?" Judge Troy Brown asked.

The first juror stood up and said, "We, the jury, find Ms. Ginger Hatchett guilty of murder in the first degree." He then sat back down.

Question: Being blind, how was Sandy able to testify in court as a suitable witness?

<u>Answer</u>: Sandy was an "ear witness" and "nose witness."
Blind people learn to use their ears, hands, and noses as
their "eyes." Sandy used both her ears and nose at the
scene of the crime.

Helicopter Splash!

A scuba diving team swam to the middle of Kentville Lake and discovered the remains of the helicopter that splashed into the lake twenty years ago. A crane was used to pull the helicopter out of the lake. Paul White stood in the middle of the shoreline and watched.

Paul looked at Kenny Grey, the first scuba diver.

"I've been telling people for twenty years the helicopter splashed in the center of the lake," Paul said, "but nobody listened."

"You're right," said Ken. "We looked near the eastern shoreline and the western shoreline."

"Twenty years ago, I was a twelve-year-old kid who happened to be the only eyewitness to the helicopter splash. Others recorded the entire event with their camera phones. I was also the only person who stood in the middle of the shoreline," Paul said.

"Both passengers got out safely and parachuted to the middle shoreline."

"I remember the incident like it was yesterday. The propellers stopped and both men parachuted to the shoreline. I'm glad nobody was hurt."

"It was on Memorial Day that year."

"Now, twenty years later, they find the helicopter in the center of the lake, just like I said it would be. Of course, nobody listens to a twelve-year-old kid."

"All the other spectators posted their recorded footage on social media. Some said it splashed near the eastern shoreline. Some said it splashed near the western shoreline."

"Every summer, for the last twenty years, some scuba divers looked in the eastern part of the lake. Some scuba divers looked on the western part of the lake. Nobody thought to look in the middle."

"Due to my being a twelve-year-old kid with no smartphone, I had no evidence proving that the helicopter splashed into the middle of the lake. That's why I was ignored."

Paul and Ken were surrounded by news reporters and cameras. A female news reporter stood next to Paul.

"I'm Shannon Choi, and I'm standing next to Paul White, the man who's been calling Kentville's anonymous tipline for years. But his calls were ignored," Shannon said while looking into the camera.

"I was ignored because I was a twelve-year-old kid with no camera phone. I was the only eyewitness to the splash. I had no evidence, only my words," Paul told Shannon.

"All of the spectators stood on one side of the lake. Some spectators recorded the helicopter splash from the eastern shoreline. Some spectators recorded the helicopter splash from the western shoreline. Paul White was the only eyewitness to the helicopter splash. He was a twelve-year-old boy with no smartphone at the time," Shannon said.

"I was also the only one who stood in the middle of the shoreline. I was so convinced that I donated my own money towards looking for the helicopter," Paul said as he looked into the news camera. "I inherited a large sum of money from an uncle."

"While some spectators claimed the helicopter splashed into the lake near the eastern shoreline, others claimed it splashed into the lake near the western shoreline. You were the only actual eyewitness and you saw it splash into the center of the lake," Shannon confirmed again.

"Why would some spectators see it splash near the eastern shoreline and others see it splash near the western shoreline?" asked Ken. "I simply don't understand."

"I can explain," Paul told Ken. Paul stood in front of the camera and explained why the spectators all seemed to see something different.

Question: Why did some spectators record the helicopter splash near the eastern shoreline and other spectators recorded it splash near the western shoreline?

<u>Answer</u>: The spectators who recorded the helicopter splash recorded only half of the lake. To the spectators on the eastern side of the lake, the helicopter appeared to splash into the lake near the western shoreline. To the spectators on the western side of the lake, the helicopter appeared to splash into the lake near the eastern shoreline. Paul, who stood in the middle of the shoreline, was the only eyewitness who saw where the helicopter splashed.

Hit Man in Hell

Lenny Panther died in a car accident due to being intoxicated while driving. He then woke up in Hell. At first, it was completely dark. Gunshots came at him from nowhere. He ran to some big rocks and hid. The rocks turned around and then formed faces.

"This ain't no hiding place!" said the biggest rock.

"Where am I?" Lenny asked.

Lenny began to have flashbacks about all the people he had shot and killed.

He then ended up being trapped in a pit filled with snakes. All the snakes continually bit him, but he couldn't die.

"I just want to die!" Lenny cried out in agony.

Lenny had flashbacks about all the people he killed by throwing them into a manmade pit filled with rattlesnakes.

He was then tied to a tree and set on fire. He burned, but he still didn't die.

"Why can't I just die?" Lenny cried out.

He had flashbacks to the time he murdered a wealthy man named Jamal Wethington. Lenny wanted Jamal's beautiful wife, Silvia. Lenny killed Jamal by inviting him on a hunting trip. While in the woods, he tied Jamal to a tree and set him on fire. Lenny's lawyer, Attorney Newt Lynch, used the argument "no witnesses, no case." Lenny was acquitted. After his acquittal, he married Silvia.

In the distance, Lenny saw Karen Humphrey, the wife of Doctor Troy Humphrey, surrounded by swarms of bees.

Lenny had flashbacks to the time Karen and he lured a young lady named Katrina Taylor to an abandoned barn.

"This barn is filled with bees," Karen told Katrina.

"Please don't throw me in there," begged Katrina. "I'm allergic to bees."

"I know you are!" shouted Karen. "Every lady who ever got pregnant by my husband has had to suffer the consequences!"

"Dr. Humphrey told me that he and you were getting a divorce. I didn't know he lied to me until after I became pregnant with our son." Katrina was terrified.

Karen kicked Katrina into the barn and quickly closed the door, trapping Katrina inside. Inside the barn, bees swarmed around Katrina as she screamed for help.

Lenny used some cinder bricks to block the front barn door while Karen used cinder bricks to block the back door. After Lenny and Karen blocked both doors, there was sudden silence.

"We're not going inside. She might be faking," Karen told Lenny.

"I hope there are no witnesses." Lenny was nervous as he looked around.

"I come from two of the wealthiest families in Kentucky. All the men in my family were lawyers who became judges. It's been that way ever since the post-civil war. All the men in my husband's family have been doctors ever since the post-civil way. I can commit murder and get away with it. Especially if they were ladies who got pregnant by married men," Karen gloated.

Karen walked to her car and returned with a briefcase.

"Here's your twenty-thousand dollars." Karen handed Lenny a briefcase.

"Thank you so much." Lenny then opened and closed the briefcase.

Lenny walked towards his car and Karen walked towards hers.

"Help me!" Karen yelled as she grabbed her chest.

Lenny ran to Karen and then called 911. When the paramedics got there, it was too late. Karen died from a heart attack.

This was the end of Lenny's flashback.

Lenny watched in horror as bees continued to sting Karen.

A beekeeper approached Lenny. The beekeeper suddenly turned into a demon.

"Welcome to Hell," the demon told Lenny.

Lenny then woke up in prison and was relieved.

The prison guard walked past all the cells.

"Time to wake up, girls!" shouted the prison guard.

"I'm so glad to see you," Lenny told him.

"You're going to die by lethal injection on Monday," the guard told Lenny.

"I'm going to be baptized on Sunday. I know that God will forgive me for what I've done."

Question: How can Lenny wake up in Hell one moment and in prison the next?

<u>Answer</u>: Lenny only dreamed about being in Hell. He was really in prison. Lenny got baptized on Sunday. He still received the death sentence on Monday.

Who's the Horse Design Thief?

Crest Woods and Tiffany Woods, Crest's daughter, visited Lexington, Kentucky for the *Spring Fling Fashion Show*. Lem Brooks and his wife, Faith, also visited Lexington for the same reason. They all stayed at a five-star hotel in downtown Lexington.

Tiffany decided to ride her motorcycle one morning. Before she rode back into the garage, she stopped and looked at a horse statue in front of the hotel. She then looked up at the beautiful blue sky.

Lem and Faith sat in their room and ate breakfast. They both looked down at the horse statue. They then looked at the white whipped cream on their fruit.

That night, Crest looked out the window at the horse statue, which was now surrounded by solar lights. After staring at the statue, he closed the curtains. Crest had a top room to himself. He had a glass ceiling and he stared at the night sky as he fell asleep.

Crest and Tiffany's chauffeur, Mrs. Sandy Alexander, drove them to the big castle on Lexington Road in Versailles,

Kentucky. Lem and Faith's chauffeur, Mr. Jack Alexander, gave them a ride to the big castle in Versailles as well. All four of them watched the fashion show.

The following year, Crest Woods, Tiffany Woods, Lem Brooks, and Faith Brooks entered their fashions in the *Spring Fling Fashion Show*.

"Welcome to Kentucky's Annual *Spring Fling Fashion Show* in the big castle in beautiful Versailles, Kentucky." Jack Alexander was the host that year.

"First up, are the designs from Ms. Tiffany Woods." Sandy Alexander was the hostess.

A male and a female model came onto the stage.

"The male model wears a sky-blue pant suit with a vest," Jack started. "His suit has brown racehorses on the vest."

The male model put on a shawl.

"His shawl is also sky-blue, with brown racehorses. The model also wears sky-blue suede shoes." Jack continued. "Thank you."

The male model exited the stage.

"The female model wears a sky-blue dress, with brown racehorses," Sandy said.

The female model put on a hooded shawl.

"The female model also wears a sky-blue hooded shawl, with brown racehorses. She is wearing flat, sky-blue dress shoes." Sandy continued. "Thank you."

The female model exited the stage.

"Next, are the designs from Mr. Lem and Mrs. Faith Brooks," Jack said.

Another male and female model came onto the stage. Tiffany gasped.

"This is odd," Jack stated. "This male model wears a white pant suit with a vest. His outfit also sports brown racehorses."

The second male model put on his shawl.

"The shawl is white, with brown racehorses." Jack stuttered, "H-he also wears white suede shoes." Jack was puzzled. "Thank you."

The second male model exited the stage.

"The female model wears a white dress, with brown racehorses." Sandy was also puzzled.

The second female model put on her shawl.

"The female model wears a white hooded shawl, with brown racehorses. She wears flat white dress shoes." Sandy looked at the female model. "Thank you."

The second female model exited the stage.

"Last, is the design by Mr. Crest Woods," Jack said.

A third male and female model come onto the stage.

"The male model wears a black pant suit with a vest." Jack was stunned. "His suit also has brown racehorses on it."

The third male model put on his shawl.

"The shawl is black, with brown racehorses." Jack struggled to speak. "He wears black suede shoes. Thank you."

The third male model exited the stage.

"The female model wears a black dress, with brown racehorses." Sandy scratched her head.

The female model put on her shawl.

"The female model wears a black shawl, again, with brown racehorses." Sandy proceeded, "She wears flat, black dress shoes. Thank you."

The third female model exited the stage.

"Who stole whose design?" Tiffany shouted. "Who's the horse design thief?"

Crest, Tiffany, Lem, and Faith all discussed where they were when they got their ideas for their designs. All four of them laughed.

Question: Who stole whose horse design?

_____

<u>Answer</u>: None of them stole another's design. All of them were in different locations when they came up with the same idea. All four of them worked on their designs together after that and became very successful.

Hospital Troll

Kentville was a small city with two hospitals. The first hospital was called *West Kentville Hospital* and the second one, *East Kentville Hospital*. West Kentville Hospital was for the poor and middle class on government medical assistance and workplace health insurance. East Kentville Hospital was for the wealthy as well as the high ranking and retired military residents of East Kentville.

It was morning, and Daphne Forest rushed her husband, John Forest, to East Kentville. John was having a heart attack. She brought John to Doctor Leonard Payne immediately.

"Doctor Payne, it's my husband's heart again." Daphne was frantic.

"I'll see him immediately," Doctor Payne told her.

***

Lee Valentine worked as an orderly at East Kentville, and he'd been in love with Daphne for years. She had the specific features that Lee wanted his woman to have.

Reverend Jesse Valentine, Lee's uncle, was the hospital chaplain.

Lee and Jesse sat together in the cafeteria.

"Daphne is a beautiful woman," Lee said.

"Daphne has a husband and adultery is a sin. There are plenty of single women here in Kentville," said Reverend Valentine.

"Daphne has the physical features that I want my woman to have. If a woman doesn't have the physical features that I want her to have, then she can't have me," Lee said.

***

Daphne and Doctor Payne talked in the hallway.

"The good news is John is at the top of the list for a heart transplant," said Doctor Payne.

"That is good news," Daphne replied.

"Until we find him a new heart, he cannot have any drama in his life. Also, he cannot be around anything that frightens him."

"I fully understand. He's terrified of rats," Daphne told the doctor.

"Just keep him in a comfortable, drama-free, and rat-free environment until he gets a new heart." Doctor Payne then patted Daphne on the shoulder.

Doctor Payne then glanced at a lady in the hallway who was drinking a cup of coffee. The lady had raggedy fingernails and continually scratched her skin.

***

It was nighttime, and John was alone in his home office, on the computer. There was a loud knock on his window. He looked outside, and someone stuck a dead rat in John's view. The rat triggered a fatal heart attack for John.

According to witnesses, the person running away from the house wore a black hoodie and a full-face mask. But they had raggedy fingernails and continually scratched their skin.

Daphne attended her husband's funeral. Angel Thacker barged into the church during the funeral and grabbed Daphne. Angel had raggedy fingernails and scratched her skin often.

"Daphne, you're going to marry my brother, Lee Valentine, today!"

"I just buried my husband. Besides, I don't have a marriage license."

"While you were in the hospital crying over your dead husband, I went into your purse and stole your driver's license! I also forged your signature on a marriage license." Angel threw Daphne's driver's license into her face.

Angel then grabbed Daphne and dragged her out of the funeral service.

The next day, Lee moved in with Daphne, his new wife.

You're my woman now," Lee said. "In order for a woman to have me, she must have the physical features I want my woman to have."

Angel knocked on the door, and Lee answered.

"I need some money!" Angel said as she stepped inside. She had raggedy fingernails and continually scratched her skin.

"Not my late husband's money," Daphne said.

"Once you married me, your money became my money," Lee said as he threw Daphne up against a wall and put his fist in her face. "Go get your purse, give Angel your ATM card, and let her have your ATM number."

Scared of Lee, Daphne complied.

The next day, two detectives were seen walking out of Doctor Payne's office. Later that night, the detectives came to Angel's house to arrest her for the rat incident. But she was dead from a drug overdose. She had a needle in her arm.

Question: How did the detectives know that Angel was both the hospital troll and John's killer?
_____

<u>Answe</u>r: Witnesses, including Doctor Payne, described both the hospital troll and John's killer as having raggedy fingernails and continually scratching their skin.

Hulk on the Roof

I held a summer day cookout in the front yard of our house. My husband, Edward, and I went inside while our four grandsons played in the front yard. Our daughters, Mia and Nile were on the front porch texting instead of watching their sons. Our two sons-in-law, Andre and Jamal were also texting and taking selfies instead of watching the children.

Edward came outside with a plate filled with hotdogs and hamburgers to put on the grill.

"Hulk on the roof!" shouted two-year-old Randy as he pointed up to the rooftop.

"A hawk?" I shouted as I grabbed my four-pound chihuahua, Naha. I didn't want her to become a hawk's dinner!

I held Naha tightly as I looked up to the rooftop. I saw Randy's *Incredible Hulk* on the rooftop.

"Who threw that up there?" I asked all four boys.

I immediately looked at Joseph. He was ten-years-old, but he was the height of a thirteen-year-old.

"Raymond did it!" shouted Joseph as he pointed to his brother, Raymond.

"Graham did it!" eight-year-old Raymond said as he pointed to his cousin, Graham.

"Randy did it!" shouted four-year-old Graham as he pointed to his two-year-old brother.

I picked up Randy, who was the size of a one-year-old, and pointed to the rooftop.

"Did you throw *Incredible Hulk* up on the rooftop?" I asked Randy.

"Yes," said Randy as he pointed up to the *Incredible Hulk* on the rooftop.

Some two-year-olds will say yes to anything.

"I guess all of you were too busy texting and taking selfies to see who threw the *Incredible Hulk* on the rooftop?" I asked our daughters and sons-in-law.

"The positive is none of the boys played in the road," said Mia.

"Of course not," I responded. "Edward and I have a six-feet-high chain-link fence in the front yard. We also have a six-feet high wooden fence in the back yard and a basketball goal for Joseph and Raymond to play with," I finished.

While the food was cooked on the grill, Edward got a ladder from the shed and got the *Incredible Hulk* off the rooftop.

"I don't know which one of you threw it up there. But don't let this happen again," Edward told Joseph as he handed the *Incredible Hulk* to him.

Joseph handed the *Incredible Hulk* to Randy.

After Edward handed the *Incredible Hulk* to Joseph, he proceeded with cooking the food. We all then ate a delicious summer day dinner.

Later that night, Edward and I stayed up to watch the news. Joseph, who had a difficult time sleeping, came into the living room.

"Grandma, I have a confession," said Joseph as he rubbed his sleepy eyes.

"Grandma, I also have a confession," Raymond said as he followed behind Joseph.

"What's the confession?" I asked.

"Raymond, Graham, and I had a throwing contest with the *Incredible Hulk,* and one of us won the contest," said Joseph.

"Randy just watched and laughed. He had nothing to do with the *Incredible Hulk* being on the rooftop," Raymond confirmed.

"We know that Randy didn't do it. He's the size of a one-year-old," Edward said.

"Do go on," I responded.

"We didn't mean for *Incredible Hulk* to end up on the rooftop." Joseph hung his head in shame. "I'm so sorry."

"I believe I know which one of you did it," I told Joseph.

"I also believe I know which one of you did it," Edward told Joseph.

"You two go back to bed, and we'll worry about it tomorrow," I told both boys.

"Good-night, Grandma and Granddad," Joseph said.

Joseph kissed Edward and me on the cheek. Raymond then kissed us both on the cheek.

Joseph and Raymond went to bed, and Edward and I continued to watch TV.

Edward and I looked at each other. We now knew who threw the hulk on the roof.

Question: Who threw the *Incredible Hulk* onto the rooftop?

_____

<u>Answer</u>: Joseph threw the *Incredible Hulk* onto the rooftop. Raymond and Graham were grounded for a week for lying. Joseph was grounded for throwing The *Incredible Hulk* onto the rooftop and for lying. No videogames for Joseph, Raymond, or Graham for a week.

In the Genes

Tom Walker was at the DNA lab with his father, Patrick Walker, and his mother, Carlita Garcia. It was nine o'clock in the morning.

"Why are you here today?" Doctor Leonard Payne asked Patrick.

"I don't believe Tom is my son. He has blond hair, and all the men in my family have red hair. Also, Carlita is Mexican American, and all the people in her family have black hair," said Patrick.

"When Tom was a baby, Patrick divorced me and took his name back. I entered divorce court as Mrs. Carlita Walker. I left as Ms. Carlita Garcia," sobbed Carlita.

"I divorced her because I thought she cheated on me, and that's why Tom was born with blond hair!" Patrick was angry.

"My mother cosigned for me to enlist in the army when I graduated from high school at seventeen," Tom told

Doctor Payne. "I'm now twenty-one, and I plan to pay for the DNA test."

"After the divorce, I've been in one failed relationship after another," Patrick admitted.

"After our divorce, I lived in one overcrowded house after another," said Carlita. "There were times when Tom had to share a bed with his cousins."

"If Tom is my son, then I will remarry Carlita. But both of my parents had red hair. Both my paternal grandparents had red hair. My maternal grandfather also had red hair, but my maternal grandmother died before I was ever born." Patrick continued, "All four of my grandparents came from Scotland. Both of my parents were each first-generation Scottish Americans."

"I'll put a swab into each of your mouths, and I'll get the results within a few hours," Doctor Payne told Patrick, Carlita, and Tom. "I'll call all of you in a few hours."

Patrick, Carlita, and Tom left. Tom drove Patrick to his house and then drove Carlita home.

Patrick, Carlita, and Tom each received a text at three o'clock that afternoon. Tom and Carlita got into the car. Tom then went to pick up Patrick.

All three of them nervously sat across the table from Doctor Payne.

"According to the DNA Test, Patrick, you test one-hundred percent positive. In other words, you're Tom's father," Doctor Payne told Patrick.

"But how?" asked Patrick. "I Have red hair. Both of my parents have red hair. Three of my grandparents have red hair."

"I went to visit my great-grandfather, Mr. Robert King, before he died." Tom pulled out some old photos and showed them to Patrick. "He gave me all these photos to keep. Included is a photo of your grandmother, my great-grandmother, Beatrice King."

"This is the first time I've ever seen a photo of my maternal grandmother. She was beautiful. Until today, I never knew what she looked like," Patrick said as he held the photos in his hands.

The photo held the answer to Tom's blonde hair. Patrick showed the photo to Carlita and Doctor Payne. Patrick then gave the photo back to Tom. Tom put the photo back into his wallet.

Patrick looked at Carlita.

"Carlita, I'm so sorry that I falsely accused you of cheating on me. I now know why Tom was born with blond hair." Patrick had sorrow in his voice.

"When we got married, you were my first and my only. I've never cheated on you. I forgive you for making such accusations." Carlita hugged Patrick.

"Will you marry me again?"

"Yes." Carlita was overjoyed.

"I want to give Mom away at the wedding!" Tom excitedly shouted.

Patrick and Tom both stood up and shook hands.

"It's a done deal, son. You can give your mom away at our wedding." Patrick hugged Tom.

Doctor Payne stood up and shook hands with both Patrick and Carlita.

"Congratulations to all of you," said Doctor Payne.

"Just think, a photo that my maternal grandfather kept for many years and a DNA test have reunited our family." Patrick openly wept.

Question: Why did Tom have blond hair?

_____

<u>Answer</u>: Tom had blond hair because his paternal great-grandmother, Mrs. Beatrice King, had blonde hair. Tom having blond hair was a recessive gene. Patrick and Carlita got remarried.

Jesse's Dream

One Sunday, after church, Lee entered his uncle Jesse's office.

"Uncle Jesse, I've been in dozens of failed relationships since high school. I guess I dump them because they don't look like Daphne. Also, they don't come from wealthy families like Daphne. After high school, why did she marry a middle-aged widower in the Marines when she was supposed to marry me?" asked Lee.

"Even after Daphne got married, you cannot keep her off your mind. As your pastor, it's my obligation to let you know that you even thinking about her is adultery."

"I know. But she's the only one who has the physical features I want my woman to have. If a woman doesn't have the features I want her to have, then she can't have me. You're also an attorney. Is there anything you can do? Can you dissolve their marriage so I can have Daphne?"

Joseph barged into the office. "Did you hear the news?"

"What news?" Jesse and Lee shouted at the same time.

"John Forest, Daphne's husband, is staying at the cancer research hospital. Since his wealthy in-laws have supported this hospital for decades, he's being treated for free," Joseph told them.

"He also receives free treatment because he's an active military person," said Jesse.

Jesse turned and looked at Lee. "That's good news. If John dies, then I can make Daphne marry you."

Ms. Bonnie Valentine entered the office. "Did all of you hear the good news?"

"Yes, Mom," responded Lee. "If John dies from cancer, then Daphne would be available for me to marry. I finally get to have the only woman I ever wanted."

"In less than a year, John will die, and you get to marry Daphne. To marry a beautiful woman from a wealthy family, is like winning the lottery," Bonnie told Lee.

Joseph grew furious. "Jesse, you're my brother. Bonnie, you're our baby sister. Lee, you're my nephew. But all of you are wrong. How dare all of you want John to die so Lee can have Daphne! Daphne wasn't interested in Lee in high school! She's not interested in Lee now!"

"I'm also an attorney," said Jesse. "I can make Daphne marry Lee. Besides, women who look like her think they're too good for men like Lee. That's judging him. If I bring up her 'ill behaviors' towards others in the past, then she'll marry Lee so none of this will be exposed."

"What do you mean?" asked Joseph.

"My exposing her 'ill behaviors' towards the working class can jeopardize her parents' and three older brothers' careers as doctors," responded Jesse as he reclined in his office chair.

A year passed, and John pulled into the driveway of his in-laws' house.

John unlocked the doors, and a masked gunman jumped into the back seat. John saw the gunman through the rearview mirror.

"Don't move!" shouted the gunman.

"What have I done?" sobbed John. "Please, whatever you want, you can have."

"My nephew wants your wife. He's been wanting her since high school."

John was horrified.

"How dare you marry the kind of woman another man needs. My nephew needs a wife, and you married the woman he needed." The gunman shot John in the back of the head.

After John's funeral, Jesse grabbed Daphne.

"My nephew needs a wife, and you will marry him today!" shouted Jesse. "By the way, I know about your 'ill behaviors' towards others in the past, and I can use that information to ruin your family's reputation and even their careers!"

At the courthouse, Daphne married Lee.

The following Sunday, Joseph entered Jesse's office, and Jesse was shaking.

"What's wrong?" asked Joseph.

"I continually have nightmares about shooting and killing a man for his lottery winnings. I then gave the other man's lottery winnings to Lee. What does that mean?"

"I've been translating dreams since we were kids. The lottery winnings represent a person."

"Make that make sense!" shouted Jesse. "Who does it represent?!"

"Think about it."

<u>Question</u>: Who did the lottery winnings represent?
_____

<u>Answer:</u> The lottery winnings represented Daphne. For some men, to marry a young, beautiful woman from a rich family is equal to winning the lottery.

John Legacy

Wanda and Wendy Morris, a set of identical twins, read a *Kentucky Wealth* magazine.

Wanda read a section titled, *Successful Singles*.

"John Legacy recently inherited $250 million from his late maternal grandparents, Peter and Christy Berry. There was a specific type of mulberry that should never be eaten, due to making people sick. Peter and Christy, who were scientists, came up with a way to use this specific type of mulberry in hair care products and perfume. Peter came up with the mulberry perfume industry. Christy came up with the mulberry hair care products industry," Wanda read.

"Is he single?" asked Wendy.

"Of course," answered Wanda. "The section he's in is titled, *Successful Singles.* The suit he's wearing in the magazine looks expensive. He's also wearing python-skin boots."

Wendy logged into her Facebook page.

"Oh, my goodness!" shouted Wendy. "According to my Facebook page, John Legacy has been spotted at the *AM/PM Buffet* restaurant in South Central Louisville! He eats there every Saturday morning."

"Why would he eat breakfast at a place like that?" asked Wanda. "That area is for working people. He should stay in East Louisville."

Maybe he's supporting working, poor people. He might be eating at *AM/PM Buffet* as a form of charity. Who knows?" responded Wendy.

"Starting this Saturday, we're going to *AM/PM Buffet* for breakfast," Wanda said.

Every Saturday morning, Wanda and Wendy went to *AM/PM Buffet* for breakfast. They stayed from 7:00 am until 10:30 am. The lunch buffet started at 11:00 am.

"After entering, we'll walk around the restaurant in a circle until we find him," said Wanda.

"Agreed. We'll walk around until we see John Legacy," Wendy agreed.

A homeless-looking man in old, tattered clothes looked up at Wanda and Wendy.

"What are you looking at, homeless man?" Wanda asked.

"Homeless people don't get to look at us!" said Wendy.

The well-dressed couple the homeless-looking man sat with gave Wanda and Wendy hostile stares.

"Oh, look. This nice couple decided to feed this homeless man," said Wanda.

"If you continue to feed homeless people, then they'll expect it all the time," Wendy told the couple.

The couple, again, gave Wanda and Wendy hostile stares.

The restaurant was filled with young, single ladies. The homeless-looking man got up to get more food from the buffet.

"Your shoes have holes in them!" shouted Wanda as she pointed to the homeless-looking man's shoes. All the other single ladies in the restaurant laughed.

Mrs. Bernice Hayden, a manager, angrily stormed out of the kitchen.

"You ladies will not treat other customers like this!" Bernice told Wanda and Wendy.

"Why do you let homeless people eat here?" Wendy asked Bernice.

"He's a paying customer," answered Bernice.

"I guess the well-dressed couple he's sitting with pays for his meals. He looks too poor to pay for his own meal to me," said Wanda.

"Looks can be deceiving," Bernice told Wanda. "If you continue to treat other customers like this, then I'll have you banned from this restaurant."

"All the men in my family are attorneys and judges. You cannot do that!" shouted Wendy.

"Many of the customers in here used their phones to videotape your behavior. Besides, our restaurant also has connections to attorneys," Bernice informed Wendy. Wanda and Wendy both got up and left.

"Whoever posted something on Facebook about John Legacy being at *AM/PM Buffet* every Saturday lied!" shouted Wendy.

"We never saw him there!" Wanda angrily agreed. "I even posted on Facebook that the person who said John Legacy was at AM/PM Buffet lied!"

"If I find the lady who posted that lie on Facebook, then I'm going to make her regret it! The only single man we saw in there was the homeless-looking man who sat with the well-dressed couple. The one wearing shoes with holes in them." Wendy was angry.

"Whoever posted that on Facebook will be so sorry she did!" shouted Wanda.

Question: Where in the restaurant was John Legacy?
_____

<u>Answer</u>: John Legacy was the homeless-looking man. He wore old, tattered clothes as well as shoes with holes in them to look poor. He simply wanted all the gold-diggers to leave him alone. The well-dressed couple were some of John's employees.

Ladies' Room Confession?

Mary Hatfield both owned and worked at the *Pillow Makers* manufacturing plant. Monday was Renee Thacker's first day.

Mary gave Renee a tour of the facility.

"My late husband, Tom Hatfield, invented the temperature pillows. There's a knob on the back of each pillow. You can make it slightly warm in the winter and slightly cool in the summer. We even make body pillows and pillows to wrap around seatbelts in vehicles," Mary told Renee.

"As far as the pillows to wrap around seatbelts in cars, do you have a warning tag on the pillow, to warn drivers to never use the pillow while driving?" Renee asked.

"Yes, we do," Mary answered. "Today, you'll work with Chesa Muang. Cetan Muang, her husband, speaks fluent English and is the repair person here. Your first task will be to sweep cotton off the floor," Mary finished.

"Can you please hand me the broom?" Renee asked Chesa.

"She's Burmese and doesn't speak English," Mary told Renee.

Renee got the broom and swept up the cotton from the floor.

The bell rang then, because it was lunchtime.

Mary and Renee spent the last ten minutes of their lunch break in the ladies' bathroom, talking. Chesa brushed her teeth while Mary and Renee talked.

"How do you like the job so far?" Mary asked Renee.

"I like it, but I don't plan to be here for long."

"Why do you say that?"

"A woman named Doreen Meadows inherited millions of dollars from her late grandparents. They were the founders of the Mulberry Hair Products Industry."

"How does Doreen Meadows' inheritance benefit you?"

Last week, I beat her up and told her that she will marry my brother, Lee Valentine, so he can have all her money. I warned her that if she doesn't marry Lee so he can have all her money, then she's going to regret it."

"I still don't see how Lee marrying Doreen will benefit you."

"After Lee marries Doreen and Doreen gives all her money to him, then Lee will give all her money to me." Renee pointed to herself. "I'm going to be a rich woman."

"I killed Tom's first wife, Charlotte, by putting Tom's heart pills into her aspirin bottle. She took his heart pills and died almost immediately. The police considered it an accidental death. A few months after Charlotte's death, Tom married me. After he died, this company became mine. I own Pillow Makers now."

The bell rang, signaling the end of the lunch break.

Chesa spoke with Cetan in Burmese while they both stood in front of a machine.

"I guess that machine is broken again," Mary observed.

Day after day, Mary and Renee shared their ladies' room confessions during the last ten minutes of their lunch breaks. At the same time, Chesa brushed her teeth.

Each day, Chesa stood at a machine and spoke with Cetan in Burmese.

"It looks like a machine breaks down every day," Renee said.

Thursday afternoon, Mary and Renee stood in the ladies' bathroom during the last ten minutes, as usual, talking as Chesa brushed her teeth.

"Doreen married Lee and gave all her money to him. Soon, Lee will share the money with me, and I'll be rich. Soon, I can quit this job!" Renee was excited.

"I'm happy for you," responded Mary as the bell rang.

Chesa and Cetan stood at another machine, speaking in Burmese.

"I guess another machine is broken?" Mary laughed.

Friday afternoon, two police officers entered the facility and handcuffed both Mary and Renee.

"I'm arresting you for murder," Officer James Reeves told Mary.

"And I'm arresting you for a physical assault," Officer Titus Rodriguez told Renee.

The officers put Mary and Renee into the backseat of their police car.

"How did you find out?" Mary asked Officer Reeves.

"Who snitched on us?" Renee asked Officer Rodriguez.

"You don't need to know," responded Officer Reeves.

Question: How did the police find out about Mary and Renee's criminal pasts?

_____

<u>Answer</u>: Chesa didn't speak English, but she understood English. Chesa was wired, but Mary and Renee never knew it. Cetan was really an undercover police officer posing as a repair person. Mary and Renee never knew Burmese.

Large Piles of Poop!

"What a large pile of poop somebody's dog left in my front yard!" Doreen Meadows shouted angrily.

"Somebody's dog got your yard too," said Katrina Williams, Doreen's next-door neighbor.

"I work from six o'clock in the morning until three-thirty in the afternoon. At five o'clock in the morning, it was still dark. But I often wake up to the strong smell of poop around three-thirty in the morning," said Doreen as she used the hose to wash away the poop.

"Toby Thurman, the man two houses down from you, draws a disability check and has section-8 housing," Katrina said. "Why does he get to have three large Rottweilers?"

"He has three Rottweilers?"

"He has two females and one male. He named the females Treasure and Jewel. The male's name is Bruno," Katrina told her.

"I'm sure my husband and I are supporting him with our tax dollars."

"It must be nice to stay out on the front porch until five o'clock in the morning, go to sleep, and then wake up at three o'clock in the afternoon."

"I'm about to take Chelsea out for her walk."

"What breed is she?"

"She's a Choodle. Her father was a Chihuahua and her mother was a Poodle. Since both of her parents were small, she'll always be small."

Doreen went into the house to get Chelsea. She put her pet on her leash and grabbed two grocery bags. She put the first grocery bag inside the second one.

Doreen began her walk up Lager Drive with Chelsea.

"Excuse me!" shouted Kelly Mangaro. "I'm tired of you letting your dog poop in our yard at three thirty in the morning! Richard and I were both late for work because we stepped in a really big pile of poop this morning and had to change shoes!"

"Ma'am, that wasn't Chelsea!" responded Doreen.

"According to Toby Thurman, you carry that bag around as a front! You let your dog poop in everybody's yards, and you never clean it up!"

"None of that is true!"

"Toby told all the neighbors that the lady with the small, black dog allows her dog to poop in everyone's yard, and she never cleans it up! He told everyone that!"

"In the morning, Kenny puts Chelsea out in our back yard, and she goes in our back yard! I take her for a walk in the evenings, and I always bring bags with me so I can clean up her poop." Doreen angrily walked up Lager Drive to the cul-de-sac.

Chelsea did her business in the cul-de-sac. Doreen used the first bag to clean up the mess. She then put the first bag into the second bag.

Doreen and Chelsea walked back down to the other end of Lager Drive.

"Excuse me, ma'am! We've got to talk!" Kendra White, another neighbor, shouted.

"What is it, Kendra?" Doreen was aggravated by this time.

"You need to stop letting your dog poop in my yard every morning! My kids were running for the bus and almost stepped in it! Their daddy spent good money on their shoes!" Kendra said. "Do you want to buy new shoes for my kids?"

"Ma'am, that wasn't Chelsea!"

"According to Toby, it was."

"I'm tired, and I don't feel like arguing." Doreen angrily marched back towards her house.

Doreen brought Chelsea into the house, took off her leash, and put a treat into her dog bowl. She then washed her hands and cooked dinner.

The next morning, Doreen and Kenny woke up at three thirty in the morning to the strong smell of poop in their front yard. Kelly and Richard also woke up to the same strong smell in their front yard. Kendra woke up to it too. Doreen and Kenny looked out their window. Kendra looked out hers and Kelly and Richard also looked outside.

Question: Who was the culprit dog owner?

<u>Answer</u>: Toby was the culprit dog owner. Small dogs, like Chelsea, produce small amounts of poop. Large dogs, like Toby's Rottweilers, produce large amounts. Kenny puts Chelsea in their backyard in the mornings. Toby lied to the neighbors about Doreen.

Legless Lizards

Doug and Roger Parks, two brothers, visited the reptile exhibit at the zoo. Sean Dillard was the reptile exhibit tour guide. Sean guided the crowd toward the exhibit with legless lizards.

"In this aquarium, are two legless lizards. Legless lizards are commonly known as skinks. The male is Lewis, and the female is Laura," Sean told the crowd.

Lewis was green and Laura was yellow. Lewis and Laura blinked at the crowd.

"How do you know they're not snakes?" asked Douglas. "Snakes are the one without legs."

"There are a few differences between snakes and legless lizards," answered Sean. "Legless lizards have holes in the side of their heads, to hear. The holes in the sides of their heads are their ears. Snakes don't have ears. They feel vibrations through their jaws."

Lewis and Laura, again, blinked their eyes.

"Look at those eyelids," said Roger.

"Also, snakes have forked tongues, and legless lizards have fleshy tongues," Sean continued.

Lewis and Laura drank from the man-made pond of clear water.

Laura winked at the crowd.

"Laura is winking at us!" shouted Roger.

"Does she like us?" Doug asked in a smart-aleck tone.

Others in the crowd laughed.

"There are six species of legless lizards throughout the world. There are the Eastern Glass Lizard, California Legless Lizard, Anguis Fragilis of Europe, Australia's Eastern-Hooded Scaly-Foot Lizard, South Africa's Cape Legless Skink, and Sheltopusik," Sean told the crowd.

"Anguis Fragilis of Europe?" Doug asked.

"This is what the British call the slow worm, because it looks more like a worm instead of a lizard. Also, it moves very slowly," Sean explained.

"What about the Sheltopusik? Where are they located?" Roger asked.

"The Sheltopusik is native to Southern Europe and Western Asia," responded Sean.

"Are skinks common in Florida?" Roger asked. "I know that in a lot of old movies, for one female to call another female a skank was a serious insult. I guess they say skank in the deep south," finished Roger.

"I've never called another human that," answered Sean. "I imagine for one person to call another person a skink would be a deep insult. I strongly suggest that nobody calls another person a skink or any other kind of animal."

Others in the crowd nodded with agreement.

"Legless lizards mainly eat crickets, spiders, grasshoppers, caterpillars, cockroaches, and other types of insects. They can also eat fruit and vegetables," Sean told the crowd next.

The crowd watched as other zookeepers threw some sliced apples into Lewis and Laura's aquarium. Lewis and Laura continued to blink their eyes as they ate their sliced apples and watched the crowd.

"Now, let's move on to the snakes," Sean said as he led the crowd to the snakes.

People in the crowd, including Doug and Roger, noticed how the snakes had forked tongues. Also, none of the snakes had ears.

"As I said, snakes don't have ears, and they feel vibrations through their jaws. In other words, their jaws are their ears," Sean told the crowd. "Snakes also use their tongues to smell."

A snake drank the water from the man-made pond of clear water.

Like the skinks, the snakes stared at the crowd through the aquarium. Of course, the snakes didn't blink.

"Snakes mainly eat birds, lizards, amphibians, and other snakes as well as mammals. We feed these snakes mice, rats, and other rodents. Really large snakes, such as pythons and anacondas, can eat deer, antelope, impalas, and other land creatures."

As one snake slept, the crowd noticed that a transparent film covered its eyes.

"I now notice the difference between snakes and legless lizards," Roger said excitedly.

"I do, too," Doug agreed.

Others in the crowd nodded.

"How many of you notice the difference between snakes and legless lizards?" Sean asked everyone in the crowd.

Everyone in the crowd raised their hands.

Question: What's another specific difference between a snake and a legless lizard?

_____

<u>Answer</u>: Lizards have eyelids, and snakes don't. Snakes have a transparent film to cover their eyes instead of eyelids. This means that lizards can blink, but snakes can't.

Main Ingredient

Doreen Meadows and Cathy Gordon entered the *Public Pillows* warehouse at 5:00 am.

"Working at *Public Pillows* seems to make you sleepy. But it doesn't," Cathy said.

"I bring my silver forty-ounce, stainless-steel portable thermos, half-filled with decaf coffee." Doreen took a big swallow.

"Decaf coffee? Why decaf?"

"Caffeinated coffee gives me heartburn." Doreen touched her chest. "Also, caffeinated coffee gives me recurring headaches."

Titus Blackbear, Cathy and Doreen's boss, approached both ladies.

"Good morning, ladies. I want you two to know that although you work ten hours a day, five days a week, the two of you complete twelve hours' worth of work in ten hours. What do you put in that coffee?" Titus asked.

"I put in hot water to the half mark. I then add two tablespoons of decaf instant coffee, two tablespoons of pure white sugar, and two tablespoons of French Vanilla powdered creamer. I stir it up, and put on the top."

"Whatever works. You two keep up the great job." Titus gave the thumbs up and then walked on to converse with other employees.

"Tiffany Walker, our supervisor, told us that our performance goal is seventy percent. Working together, we get one hundred to one hundred and forty percent most days."

"That's when you started to follow my lead." Doreen logged into the computer.

"I started to drink decaf coffee with two tablespoons of decaf coffee, two tablespoons of pure white sugar, and two tablespoons of French Vanilla powdered creamer. But I have a white cup, with *Cathy* written in purple." Cathy took a big gulp.

Tiffany approached Cathy and Doreen.

"Today, ladies, you two will be working on the pillows going to all the *Sunshine Inn* motels. Since *Sunshine Inn* motels are the cheapest motels around, the pillows don't have to be as fluffy. Fill them up to only seventy percent capacity," Tiffany instructed.

Tiffany handed Cathy a piece of paper.

"Today, we need ninety *Sunshine Inn* pillows. After that, I need for you to make one hundred pillows for the *Golden Years Assisted Living Facility* and one hundred pillows for the *Happy Place Assisted Living Facility*."

Cathy and Doreen both pulled out their mobile phones and took a picture of the paper. They then put their phones away.

"Okay, we need ninety pillows for the *Sunshine Inn* motels. We need one hundred pillows for *Golden Years Assisted Living Facility*. Afterwards, we need one hundred more pillows for the *Happy Place Assisted Living Facility*. I got it," Cathy repeated to Tiffany.

"Thank you very much, ladies." Tiffany took back the paper and then walked away.

Jason McCoy rode by on his forklift. He stopped to greet Cathy and Doreen.

"Good morning, ladies," Jason said before he took a big gulp of his energy drink.

"How can you drink energy drinks?" Doreen asked Jason.

"Like this." Jason took another gulp. "How can you drink decaf coffee, and still have energy?"

"Caffeinated coffee gives me heartburn and headaches. I need to go with what works. Besides, energy drinks give me the jitters. I feel like a mouse in a snake pit."

"We're all different." Jason took another gulp of his energy drink and drove away.

Cathy and Doreen used the pillow stuffing machines to stuff the pillows to seventy percent capacity. When each screen said *filled to capacity,* they each turned off their machine. They then used a sealer to seal the opened end of the pillow shut.

Cathy and Doreen were done with the *Sunshine Inn* pillows before lunch, at eleven o'clock. After lunch, they started on the pillows for the assisted living facilities.

Cathy and Doreen had all the pillows done and put into boxes before three o'clock. Jason had all the boxes loaded onto the truck before three-fifteen.

At three-twenty, Cathy and Doreen were cleaning up. Jason stopped his forklift and started chatting with them.

"All three of us working together got a twelve-hour job done in ten hours," Jason said.

"All of us had that one ingredient in our drinks that helped us too," Doreen said.

Question: What was the one ingredient that gave all three of them extra energy?

<u>Answer</u>: Sugar. Pure white sugar was in their drinks.

"Much That is Given"

Kobe Meadow was found in his car, dead from a gunshot to the head. Everyone knew that.

Michelle Fawcett did it. Michelle was represented by Attorney Newt Lynch.

Michelle winked at the jurors. All twelve jurors were intrigued with Michelle's beauty.

Kobe's wife, Doris, and his daughter, Mrs. Doreen (Meadow) Bivins, were also in the courtroom. Their attorney was Attorney Ned McCoy.

Attorney McCoy stood in front of the twelve male jurors. "Ms. Michelle Fawcett is guilty of Kobe Meadow's murder. She shot him in the head as he sat in his car, and she had no reason to kill him." Attorney McCoy then sat down.

Attorney Lynch then stood in front of the jurors. He handed the first juror a piece of paper for all of them to read and pass around.

"Mr. Kobe Meadow was a registered sex-offender,"
Attorney Lynch began. He then handed the paper to Judge
Roy Houston.

Attorney Lynch proceeded with his argument. "Ms.
Michelle Fawcett had a twenty-three-year-old son, Andre
Fawcett, who was murdered last month, and he left
behind an infant daughter named Andrea." Attorney Lynch
pointed towards Gail Cellar, the baby's mother. Holding
Andrea, Gail stood up and allowed everyone else to look at
them. She then sat back down.

"Mrs. Doreen Meadow Bivins married Mr. Ron Bivins, who
died and left here with twenty-million dollars. Ron was an
inventor and that's how he became very rich. He also
came from a family of old money, so to speak." Attorney
Lynch pointed towards Doreen. "After Ron's death,
Doreen decided to allow her father—a registered sex-
offender—and her mother, Doris, to live with her in her
late husband's mansion."

"Objection!" shouted Attorney McCoy. "What does any of
this have to do with Michelle shooting and killing Kobe?"

"I'm about to get to that," responded Attorney Lynch.

"Let Attorney Lynch speak," Judge Houston told Attorney McCoy. "You had your turn."

Frustrated, Attorney McCoy sat back down.

"Michelle's son is deceased; Andrea and Gail need a safe place to live. Everyone in Michelle's

church family agreed that Doreen's house would be the best place for Andrea to live. But Andrea cannot live there as long as Kobe lived there. Michelle doesn't want Andrea sharing a house with a registered sex-offender."

Doris stood up. "My husband received counseling after he molested our daughters! He doesn't do that anymore! We all received counseling!"

"Mrs. Meadow, one more outburst and I'll declare this a mistrial!" shouted Judge Houston.

With tears in her eyes, Doris sat back down and remained quiet.

"Each of you are to read Luke 12:48 and consider a passage in that chapter." Attorney Lynch opened a Bible and handed it to the jurors. Each juror read it and nodded.

The first juror handed the Holy Bible back to Attorney Lynch. He handed the Bible to Judge Houston. Judge Houston read it and nodded.

"This is a city filled with Bible-belted people. Everyone in here should agree with Luke 12:48. Even Doreen, who's been in the church since she was two weeks old," said Judge Houston.

Soon after, the jurors went into the chambers to discuss the verdict. They came out within five minutes.

"Have you reached a verdict?" asked Judge Houston.

The first juror stood up. "We, the jury, find Ms. Michelle Fawcett not guilty."

Judge Houston looked at Michelle. "Ms. Michelle Fawcett, you're free to go."

Judge Houston looked at Doreen. "Mrs. Bivins, you will provide for Gail and Andrea. Remember Luke 12:48." Judge Houston pounded his gavel. "Court is adjourned!"

"I know the twelve jurors found Michelle not guilty because they were intrigued with her beauty," Doris sobbed to Attorney McCoy. "I also know what's in Luke 12:48."

Question: What's in Luke 12:48?

_____

<u>Answer:</u> Luke 12:48 reads, "But he that knew not, and did commit things worthy of stripes, shall be beaten with few stripes. For unto whomever much is given, of him shall be much required: and to whom men have committed much, of him they will ask the more." (King James Version).

Attorney Lynch and Judge Houston focused on the passage, "For unto whomever much is given, of him shall be much required:"

Mysterious Creatures, Where are They?

Kyle Little and John Rock went all over the United States pursuing mysterious creatures. They visited Eastern Kentucky, in search of Bigfoot. They traveled to the Florida Everglades, looking for the skunk ape. They even traveled to New York State, looking for the Lake Champlain creature. Both men each invested their entire inheritance in pursuing these mysterious creatures.

While in Florida, a Seminole Tribe Leader named Titus Gator approached Kyle and John.

"If you two are looking for the skunk ape, then you're not alone," Titus told them.

"Who are you?" Kyle asked Titus.

"I'm Titus Gator, a Seminole Tribe leader. We've been aware of this creature's existence for centuries," Titus told them.

"If this thing has existed for centuries, then why don't we see it? Why can't we get photos of it or get it on video?" asked John.

"If people were suddenly pursuing you with picture cameras, video cameras, and camera phones, what would you do?" Titus asked.

Kyle and John looked at each other. They then rubbed their chins.

"Think about it," Titus said as he walked away.

Kyle and John traveled to Lake Champlain in New York State, to pursue the Lake Champlain creature. Their attempt to find the creature failed.

Karen Jones, a park ranger, approached Kyle and John.

"I'm guessing you're here to get photos of Champy," Karen said.

"Who's Champy?" Kyle asked Karen.

"She's the mysterious creature who lives in Lake Champlain. People have been coming here for decades with picture cameras, video cameras and camera phones, trying to get photographs of her. She simply wants to be left alone." Karen was frustrated.

"How would you know?" John asked Karen.

"I belong to the Algonquin Tribe, and we've been aware of this creature's existence for centuries. We simply choose to leave them alone and not harass them. In fact, the first group of European settlers were scared away by this lake creature. This is the reason why we choose to protect them," Karen told Kyle and John.

Exhausted and frustrated, Kyle and John both got into their RV and drove away.

Kyle and John stopped in a rural community in Eastern Kentucky. With their camera phones in their hands, they walked towards the woods.

"I guess you're pursuing Bigfoot?" asked James Hartwell, a local resident.

"And you are?" asked Kyle.

"I'm James Hartwell. I just returned to Kentucky after serving thirty years in the Marines. From what I see, outsiders continue to come here looking for Bigfoot," James observed.

"What do you know about Bigfoot?" John asked.

"My ancestors were slaves here. They saw these creatures all the time."

"Do you have photos to prove it? Did they keep journals?" John asked James.

"Slaves never owned cameras. Also, slaves never learned to read and write."

"How do you know that your ancestors saw these creatures?"

"Folks around here have been talking about Bigfoot for generations."

"Why didn't any of your ancestors chase after it?"

"My ancestors worked from sunup to sundown. After the work was done, they tended to their own families. We had no time for chasing after Bigfoot. Folks around here choose to leave the creature alone. We don't bother it, and it doesn't bother us."

LeeAnn McCoy walked up with a shotgun and pointed it at Kyle and John.

Billy McCoy, a man with long, blond hair, also approached Kyle and John with a shotgun.

"You men had better get back into your RV and drive away!" LeeAnn was angry. "We had better not see you around here again!"

"You'd better do what my wife says," Billy told Kyle and John. "Don't die looking for fortune and fame."

Kyle and John got into the RV, and Kyle quickly drove away.

"If these mysterious creatures exist, then why don't we see them?" asked John.

"What would we do if people suddenly pursued us with picture cameras, video cameras, and camera phones?" asked Kyle.

Question: If these mysterious creatures exist, then why do pursuers like Kyle and John never see them?

<u>Answer</u>: These mysterious creatures learned to hide. If people suddenly pursued you with picture cameras, video cameras, and camera phones, then you would hide too.

Mysterious Lake Creatures in Kentucky Lake

Lewis McGuinness and his wife, Laura, traveled to Kentucky all the way from Loch Ness, Scotland. In the morning, they sat in front of a large window in the inn and ate breakfast. A large creature slowly appeared out of the lake and then quickly swam away.

"Do they have a lake creature here too?" Laura, in her thick Scottish accent, asked Daisy McCoy, the hostess.

"The people around here have been knowing about these mysterious lake creatures for centuries," Daisy replied in her thick, southern accent.

"I'll bet you also receive lots of tourism because of this, my lady," Lewis told Daisy.

"Mainly in the spring, summer and autumn," said Daisy as she poured her guests more coffee. "We have no tourists during the winter. My husband, Floyd, and I get temporary jobs nearby during the winter months."

"The McCubbin family here in town found us through one of those Ancestry searches. They then invited us here. Lewis and I came here to meet our distant relatives here in America," Laura told Daisy.

"I know the McCubbin Family," Daisy said. "Floyd and I work in one of their stores during the winter months."

"The McCubbin family owns stores?" Lewis asked Daisy.

"The McCubbin Family owns food-chain stores in town, in nearby towns and up in Louisville."

"For decades, we've been hearing stories about relatives going to America to live. They found us through some Ancestry search, like we said. Now, we're here." Lewis knocked on the table.

"We're so glad to have you here. When you return to Scotland, please tell everyone about us. We would enjoy the tourism. Our inn is open through spring, summer, and autumn."

Lewis and Laura spent the rest of the morning on the front porch. Titus Blackfoot, a Native-American man, sat on the shoreline, reading the Bible. Again, a large creature slowly appeared out of the lake and then quickly swam away. Titus was unsurprised.

Lewis and Laura rose from the porch and approached Titus.

"You seem to be unsurprised by this mysterious lake creature," Lewis said.

"I've been looking at this lake all my life. My parents brought me to this lake when I was first born. I've been looking at what you call mysterious creatures since I was a baby," Titus said as he closed his Bible and stood up.

"I'm Lewis McGuinness, and this is my wife, Laura. We're visiting from Loch Ness, Scotland."

"I'm Titus Blackfoot. My parents wanted me to have a name from the Bible."

Titus shook hands with both Lewis and Laura.

"I hear stories of Scotland having the Loch Ness Monster. You call her Nesse?"

"I'm sure every lake in the world has creatures living in it. They just choose to avoid us. Or hide from us destructive people," Lewis said with a chuckle.

"If I were a lake creature, then I would hide from people too," Titus agreed.

"My distant relative, Sheila McCubbin, told us about this mysterious lake creature. That's why we're here visiting Kentucky Lake," said Laura. "Can I ask how other tourists found out about your mysterious lake creature?"

"In the mid-2000s, a lady up in Louisville posted a story on a social media page called, *Stories, Legends, and Myths of Kentucky*. Ever since she posted the story of our mysterious lake creature, tourists have been coming from all over the United Sates and the world."

Titus stood in the shallow part of the lake. The creature swam up to Titus and allowed him to pet her. She then slowly swam away.

"I know what this mystery creature is!" Laura was excited.

"I do, too!" shouted Lewis.

"Let's keep this our secret. The tourism brings lots of financial revenue to our small city." Titus put his index finger vertically over his lips and then smiled.

Question: What was this mysterious lake creature?

<u>Answer</u>: The mysterious lake creature was a large species of catfish. The largest catfish (on record) caught in Kentucky Lake was one-hundred-twelve pounds. This was the height and size of a preteen. The social media post consisted of a woman who caught a catfish that was almost ninety pounds. It was said this catfish was four-and-a-half feet long.

Orange Wedding

It was the first Saturday in June. All of the town's people were gathered in a large chapel in Clarksville, Tennessee.

Davis Stamos stood at the altar, wearing an orange tuxedo, orange tie, and orange shoes. He also wore a white top hat with an orange rim.

Alexa Bealer, the organist, played *Here Comes the Bride* as Kim Zane entered. Kim walked down the aisle in a white dress. She held orange and white flowers. She also wore orange jewelry, orange hair accessories, and orange shoes. Kim was escorted down the aisle by her father, Mr. Hal Smithers.

Kim then stood next to Davis.

"Today, we gather on this first Saturday in June, to witness the unity of Mr. Davis Stamos and Ms. Kim Smithers." Reverend Jung Choi stood in front of the podium.

Davis and Kim turned to face each other.

"Who gives this woman to be married?" Jung looked at Hal.

"I do." Hal then sat down next to his wife, Mrs. Kathy Smithers.

"Kim has always wanted a "Tennessee orange" wedding," Kathy whispered to Hal.

"Nothing is too good for our only daughter," Hal whispered back. "We had five boys, and then Kim came along. She's our only princess. If she wants an orange wedding, then she can have one."

All of the best men wore white suits, but they wore orange ties and orange shoes.

The maids-of-honor and matrons-of-honor wore orange dresses. They also wore white jewelry, white hair accessories, and white shoes.

Jung stood with the Bible in his hand.

"If anyone objects to these two being joined in holy matrimony, then speak now or forever hold your peace." Jung looked around.

Hal stood up and gave an intimidating look. Nobody said anything. Hal sat back down.

"We'll proceed with the wedding." Jung looked at Davis. "Do you, Davis Stamos, promise to have Kim Smithers to be your lawfully wedded wife? Do you promise to love, honor, and care for her? For better or worse? For richer or poorer? Through sickness and through health? Until death do you part?"

"I do," Davis said without hesitation.

Jung looked at Kim. "Do you, Kim Smithers, promise to have Davis Stamos as your lawfully wedded husband? Do you promise to love, honor, and care for him? For better or worse? For richer or poorer? Through sickness and through health? Until death do you part?"

"I do." Kim cried happy tears.

"I now pronounce you husband and wife." Jung looked at Davis. "You may kiss the bride."

Davis and Kim embraced in a long kiss.

"You're now looking at Mr. and Mrs. Stamos." Jung looked at the congregation. "The reception will be held in the fellowship hall at the back of the church. All of you are invited. There's plenty of food for everyone."

Everyone ate the delicious meal prepared for them. All of the adults drank orange sodas. All of the children drank Tang orange juice. The cake was white with orange flowers. The groom on the cake held an orange football with the *Tennessee Volunteers* logo on it. The bride on the cake held an orange basketball with the *Tennessee Volunteers* logo on it.

When it was time for Kim to throw the bouquet, all of the single, divorced, and widowed women stood behind Kim. Mrs. Jane Brown, a sixty-year-old widow, caught the bouquet.

Kim sat in a chair and allowed Davis to remove the orange garter from her leg.

"I plan to catch the garter. Your mother died last year, so that makes me a widower." Mr. Kwang Choi, Jung's father, walked onto the floor.

"You have my blessing," Jung said.

Davis threw the garter, and Mr. Kwang Choi caught it.

Mr. Choi said something to Jung in Korean. Both laughed.

Jung looked at Davis and Kim. "My father said that you two did something for each other on your special day. I'll recite it in a one-line poem."

Davis and Kim looked at each other, looked at each other's attire, and laughed.

Question: What did Davis and Kim do for each other?

<u>Answer</u>: *Davis wore Tennessee orange for Kim. She wore Tennessee orange for him.*

Phone Call

Jacob Meadows and his twins—Doreen and Jacobi—traveled to Perlowski, New York to visit the twins' maternal grandparents. Doreen and Jacobi called them Grandma and Grandpa Reeg. Jacob and the twins arrived on Wednesday for an early Thanksgiving dinner.

While Doris Reeg prepared the dinner, Frank Reeg and Jacob talked in the garage. The twins stayed in the kitchen to help their grandmother prepare for dinner.

"Esther married an Air Force officer named Paul Pendleton. She wanted all the amenities that comes with being married to a high-ranking military man," said Frank, informing Jacob about his ex-wife.

"When she divorced me to marry Max Fields, I told her that if she stood by my side and supported me, then I'd become an officer someday. I simply needed the support of a wife."

"You were her first husband. She divorced you to marry Colonel Max Fields, who died from liver cancer two years later."

"Some women want to enjoy the amenities that come with being married to a high-ranking military man. But they don't want to put forth the work and effort it takes to help him get there. She wanted all those nice things *now*—not have to wait for them to come."

"Paul has no knowledge of your existence or the twins' existence. He married Esther, believing he married a beautiful widow who never had children. He also believes he's her second husband. He doesn't know otherwise."

"I'm sure that his knowing the truth could destroy their marriage." Jacob looked around the garage and saw lots of chewing tobacco.

"I guess Paul chews lots of tobacco?" Jacob asked as he picked up a pack of tobacco.

"He chews it all the time," Frank said.

"I used to smoke cigarettes, but I had to eventually quit. It wasn't easy, but I needed to make sacrifices so I could support the twins by myself."

"There's a passage in a song that goes, 'every man wants to die a happy man'. We'll let Paul live and die a happy man." Frank took the chewing tobacco out of Jacob's hands.

"Allowing him to believe he married a widow with no children makes him a happy man?"

"Paul wants to be a happy man with a happy life. Never knowing about your and the twins' existence will make that possible."

"Time to come in and eat!" shouted Jacobi as he stuck his head out of the kitchen door.

Everyone ate their Thanksgiving dinner at two o'clock that afternoon.

After dinner, Doreen and Jacobi helped their grandmother clear the table and wash the dishes. Doris washed and Doreen rinsed. Jacobi dried and put away the dishes.

The landline phone rang, and Doris answered it. She had a disturbed look on her face.

Jacob and Frank rose from the table.

"Is everything okay?" Frank asked.

"I'm sorry to say this, but Jacob and the twins must leave now," answered Doris.

"You said that we can spend the night and leave tomorrow morning," Doreen said sadly.

"I know, but plans have changed. All of you must leave now."

"Lucky for us, we kept our luggage in the car," said Jacob.

"Can we stay at the Perlowski Motel and leave tomorrow?" asked Jacobi.

"All of you need to leave the village immediately," Doris told them in a sad voice.

"It's a four-hour drive back, and it's getting dark soon," Jacob said.

"I pray that you get home safely," was all Doris could say.

Jacob and the twins left immediately after the phone call.

"Why did we have to leave immediately?" asked Doreen.

"None of this makes any sense," said Jacobi.

"I'll explain to you two tomorrow," Jacob said as he drove through the night.

<u>Question</u>: Why did Jacob and the twins have to leave immediately after the phone call?

_____

<u>Answer</u>: The twins' birthmother, Esther, was on the phone. Paul and she were due to arrive at the house on Wednesday evening instead of Thursday afternoon. Due to Jacob and the twins' sacrifices and the Reegs' secret-keeping, Paul never found out about Esther's kids and first husband. Many years later, Paul died of mouth cancer, and he died a happy man.

Renita's Dream

Renita Meade, Doreen Meadows, and Karen Dixon sat in the breakroom eating their lunches and talking. Karen sat across the table from Doreen.

Renita pulled out her phone and showed her high school photos to Doreen and Karen.

"When I was in the ninth and tenth grades, my boyfriend was Vincent Madison. Vincent was in twelfth grade when I was in tenth grade. At the end of my tenth-grade year, he graduated from high school and enlisted in the army." Renita looked sad.

"Were you heartbroken?" Doreen asked.

"I was until I met Lorenzo Hernandez. I went to both junior prom and senior prom with Lorenzo." Renita showed photos on her phone. "He enlisted in the Air Force after high school."

"I remember him," Doreen said. "I wonder how he's doing these days."

"He now lives in Okinawa, Japan. He's engaged to marry a young Okinawan lady." Renita put her phone away and finished her lunch.

"I hear that Okinawan women are extremely beautiful," Doreen said. "There are men in my family who enlisted in the military and lived in Okinawa, Japan."

"You're now happily married to Kevin Meade, and you're pregnant with a girl," Karen excitedly mentioned.

"I've been having a recurring dream." Renita sounded concerned.

"What was the dream about?" Doreen and Karen asked at the same time.

"A man was following me around. He wore a blue military uniform," Renita said.

"What else?" Karen was curious.

"On one occasion, I was pumping gas into my van, and he popped out of nowhere."

"What do you mean by 'popped out of nowhere'?" Karen was now concerned.

"It was like he magically popped out of nowhere," Renita answered.

"Doreen, both of your grandmothers and you have the ability to translate dreams." Karen looked across the table. "What does Renita's recurring dream mean? Is she being stalked? Is she being followed?"

"None of the above. What her dream means is that somebody's thinking about her," Doreen responded. "Somebody from her past is thinking about her."

"What about when he popped out of nowhere?" Karen asked.

"What that means is that she suddenly popped into his mind," Doreen answered.

"I'm not being stalked, and I'm not being followed." Renita was relieved. "I'm so glad you can interpret dreams."

"I can't interpret all dreams. I wish I could, but I can't." Doreen sounded disappointed.

"You being able to interpret this dream has brought me a great deal of relief." Renita sighed.

"How did you find out you were able to interpret dreams?" Karen curiously asked Doreen.

"In the past, I had a recurring dream that Aunt Joy wore a white wedding dress and ended up at the end of a road. Aunt Joy then got a divorce. Scott, her ex-husband, was a player, anyway. While they were married, multiple women called Joy to tell her that they had a baby by Scott," Doreen said.

"Joy divorcing Scott was a wise thing," Karen said. "Joy would be paying child support if she were to have stayed married to him."

"You're right," Doreen and Renita both responded.

"After my aunt got her divorce, I stopped having that dream," Doreen said.

"What other dreams did you have?" Karen was curious.

"I had a dream that Uncle Roy won thirty-three-million dollars in the lottery and kept all of his money in the basement. There was one window in the basement that was slightly opened," Doreen said.

"What in the world does that mean?!"

"In dreams, a basement represents secrets. A slightly opened window signifies that only a few people know that secret."

"How did your uncle keep his lottery winnings a secret?" Karen asked.

"Uncle Roy paid so much money to keep it out of the media. The only people in the family who knew about his winnings were my grandparents. He agreed to get the lump sum."

"Although I'm happily married, I know who was thinking about me." Renita laughed.

"We do too." Doreen and Karen spoke at the same time.

Question: Who was thinking about Renita?

<u>Answer</u>: Lorenzo Hernandez was thinking about Renita.

Lorenzo was in the Air Force, and they wore blue uniforms.

When a Blessing Becomes a Curse

"I just won one-hundred-million dollars in the Kentucky Lottery," Bo McCoy excitedly told his coworker, Pierre Beauchamp.

"You must speak in a whisper," Pierre whispered in a thick Jamaican accent as he nervously looked around at the others in the breakroom.

"I'm going to take the lump sum. That should round up to fifty-million after taxes, fees, and hush money I have to pay to these news stations."

"Here in Kentucky, lottery winners are allowed to remain anonymous. You no longer have to pay hush money to the news stations. After work, I'll give you a ride to the lottery building so you can cash in your ticket."

"Thank you so much. I'll use a portion of the money to bring the rest of your family here from Jamaica. All of you can work for me. All of you will receive free food and shelter. I'll also pay all of you a hundred dollars a day. You do all of the repairs here. You can become my repair person."

"My family and I lived in extreme poverty back in Jamaica, so that sounds great."

"When I have your entire family brought here, I'll help all of them gain citizenship. As long as all of you work for me, I'll provide all of the adults in your family free career training."

"I have three younger sisters who want to become nurses. Can you help them too?"

"Deal." Bo shook hands with Pierre.

After work, Pierre drove Bo to the lottery building in East Louisville.

"I plan to have my money transferred to my account in Oldham County, Kentucky so nobody in my family knows about this. I will then buy a mansion in Oldham County. People I haven't seen in over twenty years would be knocking on my door begging for money if they found out about this," Bo said to Pierre.

"Didn't you have a nephew who threatened you for money? You gave him your entire paycheck because he threatened to set your house on fire with you and your kids in it if you didn't give him some money."

"Your wife and you gave me half of your paychecks for six months. Angel and I appreciated that. The bad news is that he died from a drug overdose the next day." Bo hung his head with sadness.

"I'm so sorry to hear that." Pierre was sympathetic.

"Angel, the twins, and I will live in the mansion. Peola, my daughter, can now attend nursing school. Peyton, my son, can now train to become an electrician."

"I'm glad to hear the twins have positive pursuits."

"Angel can now train to become a certified Financial Advisor and Tax Preparer."

"What are you going to do for yourself?"

"I'm going to just be lazy. Rest, relax, and channel surf all day."

"Okay," Pierre responded.

Bo and his family lived in a mansion in Oldham County. Pierre, his parents, his three younger sisters and one younger brother all worked for Bo. The women in Pierre's family did the housecleaning, laundry, and cooking. Pierre's father and brother did all the yardwork and Pierre did the home repairs. Angel paid Pierre and his relatives a hundred dollars each day, as promised.

Peola attended nursing school during the day. Pierre's three younger sisters, Silvia, Vivian, and Delilah attended nursing school at night. Peyton attended electrician school during the day. Pierre's younger brother, James, did yardwork during the day and attended electrician school at night. Pierre and his family became Bo's new extended family.

Bo spent his days eating, sleeping and channel surfing. He only got up to use the bathroom.

Bo died from a severe heart attack, and Angel called Doctor Enrique Garcia.

"His lack of exercise caused a clot in his legs. The clots traveled to his heart and caused the heart attack," Doctor Garcia sadly told Bo's family and extended family.

"Bo was blessed to win the lottery. It also blessed us all. But this blessing also became his curse." Pierre cried for Bo.

Question: How did Bo's blessing become his curse?

<u>Answer:</u> The lottery money caused Bo to become lazy and dependent on others. This is what many call, "The Lottery Curse."

Who's Richer Than Whom?

Earlene Wells visited her cousin, Tom Simpson, to see his newly renovated garage.

"Tom, I really like your garage." Earlene looked around in amusement. "You even have a full bathroom in here. I remember seeing your garage on the *Extreme Garage Makeover* episode. I can live here if the rent is fair."

"With you being family, I'll charge you five-hundred a month in rent."

"That sounds fair to me." Earlene shook Tom's hand. "Paul Wells, my late husband, left me a modest inheritance. His children—Linda, Logan, and Lionel—received the land, house, and construction business."

Earlene happily pulled out five-hundred dollars and gave it to Tom. Tom put it into his wallet.

"Again, my condolences to your stepchildren and you." Tom took off his baseball cap.

"Thank you." Earlene continued to look around. "You have a fully furnished bathroom in one corner, a kitchen in the other, and a futon bed in a third corner. The fourth corner has a dining area. I even like the big screen TV mounted on the wall."

Earlene got two suitcases out of the bed of her pick-up truck and brought them into the garage. She put her items into the drawers in the third corner of the garage.

"I'm about to go inside and get ready for work tomorrow. It takes me twenty minutes to drive to my boss's house in East Louisville."

"Do you still work for Lloyd Daniels, the owner of *Daniels' Real Estate*?"

"Yes, I do," Tom responded. "And he's still unsatisfied with everything he has."

"Your boss lives in a house big enough for six families. He has a three-story house with an elevator. His wife, Kara, and he buy new vehicles every year. In the summertime, they go swimming in the lake behind their house. Why is he dissatisfied?"

"My boss complains that he doesn't have enough. He wants more."

"I feel sorry for people like him."

"You have a good night, and lock up." Tom walked out of the garage.

The next morning, Tom was doing yardwork for Lloyd.

"I hear that your cousin, Earlene Wells, lives in your garage now?" Lloyd asked Tom.

"She's a widow, and she received a modest inheritance from her late husband."

"Why would you make a widow live in a garage?"

"My garage was recently renovated. Didn't you see the *Extreme Garage Makeover* episode last month? It even has a full bathroom in it. Besides, Earlene is a humble person."

"Why didn't she go to court to get Paul's land, house, and construction business? She would've been as rich as me if she did that."

"She had no interest in Paul's land, house, or construction business. She received a modest inheritance, and she works at a call center. She's happy."

"Kara and I have six children to continue the family business and take care of us when we get old. How many children does Earlene have?"

"She had two daughters from her first late husband, Troy Moore. Troy was killed in combat. He fought in Desert Storm. Both girls, Myra and Tara, followed in their birthfather's footsteps and enlisted in the army."

"I feel sorry for people like her."

Tom said nothing as he continued with his yardwork.

With a dissatisfied look on his face, Lloyd looked around.

"Is everything okay?" Tom stopped doing his yardwork.

"I just wish I had a bigger yard and more land. I also wish I had a bigger lake and bigger fish swimming around in the lake. That would be nice. Then, I'd be happy."

"That might be more land for me to maintain."

"You could manage it. I just wish I had more."

Again, Tom said nothing. He simply returned to doing his yardwork.

Later that evening, Earlene hung up her *Employee of the Month* portrait.

"Congratulations!" Tom shouted. "You won employee of the month again!"

"I'm so happy with the way my life is going and for everything I have!"

"I believe you're richer than my boss."

Question: How could Earlene possibly be "richer" than Lloyd?

<u>Answer</u>: Earlene was "richer" than Lloyd because Earlene was happy with everything she had. No matter what Lloyd had, he always wanted more.

She Spoke His Language

There was almost a car collision on Alex Avenue. Feeling dizzy, Toby Oakdale got out of the car and stood beside his car. Officers James Reeves and Tito Garcia helped Toby get onto the sidewalk and sit down. Officer Reeves used his phone to call 911.

"What is your name and address?" Officer Reeves asked Toby.

Toby didn't respond.

Officer Garcia spoke to Toby in Spanish, and Toby didn't respond.

"I spent ten years in the army," Officer Reeves told Officer Garcia. "I spent five years as military police in Germany."

"I also spent ten years as military police in the army, and I lived in Germany for five years," Officer Garcia responded.

Both officers spoke to Toby in German, and Toby still never responded.

Mary Boston, an onlooker, looked at the officers and laughed.

"May I please communicate with him?" Mary asked the officers.

"Who are you?" Officer Garcia asked.

"I'm Mary Boston, and I believe I can communicate with him."

"More power to you." Officer Garcia allowed Mary through the yellow police tape line so she could communicate with Toby.

"Hurry up!" Officer Reeves shouted. "The ambulance is on their way."

"Here's a pen and writing pad. Take as much information as you can." Officer Garcia handed the items to Mary.

Mary approached Toby and introduced herself to Toby in a language he understood. Toby excitedly responded to Mary. When the ambulance arrived, Mary handed the pen and writing pad back to Officer Garcia.

"His name is Toby Oakdale, and he lives on this street, Alex Avenue. The other driver ran a stop sign because she was texting while driving. He slammed on his brakes really quickly, so not to hit the side of her car. Not realizing what happened, she continued to drive down the street," Mary told the officers and paramedics.

The paramedics put Toby onto the stretcher and into the back of the ambulance. They then drove away with their sirens blasting.

Professor Derek Pratt approached Mary. "Mary, I'm so pleased with what I saw." Professor Pratt patted Mary on the back. "Not everyone can pick up on that language."

"I learned from the best." Mary did a curtsy.

"I plan to retire soon. My wife and I want to spend our golden years traveling around the United States on a riverboat," Professor Pratt told Mary. "You have a teaching degree. I hope you can take my place at the university. I'll give you an outstanding reference."

"I can't say no to that!" Mary sounded excited.

"Will nine o'clock Monday be too soon?" Professor Pratt handed Mary a business card.

"That sounds perfect!" Mary excitedly took the business card.

"When you become a professor at the university, I want to take classes," Officer Reeves told Mary. "Those of us in law enforcement need to learn this language."

"I want to enroll in your classes, too," Officer Garcia told Mary.

"Since the mayor announced that our city has a budget surplus, then the police department should have as many police officers as possible enroll in your class," Officer Reeves said.

"With so many new prospective students, you might have a job on Tuesday." Professor Pratt was amused. "You don't want to let down your future students."

The following Monday, Mary visited Toby at the hospital. She told him she got the job, and he was so happy for her. Toby also spoke with his parents on his mobile phone through texts. Toby put his phone on snapchat so his parents could meet Mary.

"You're a hero to our son," Mrs. Maggie Oakdale told Mary. "Not everyone can speak in his language. I'm so glad you were there."

"I'm also glad you were there," Mr. Gordon Oakdale intervened.

"I'm happy I was there, too. I don't get to use this language every day," Mary told Mr. and Mrs. Oakdale. "You take care of yourselves." Mary handed the phone back to Toby. Toby continued to snapchat with his parents in his language. Mary patted Toby on his back, grabbed her purse, and left.

Question: What language did Toby speak?

_____

<u>Answer</u>: Toby spoke in sign language. He was born deaf.

Surprise Guest

Daphne Fern and Paul Williams just got married. Neither Paul nor Daphne had much money. Daphne's aunt, Charlene Fern, decorated her basement to look like a honeymoon suite. Paul and Daphne spent their first month of marriage at Daphne's Uncle Neo and Aunt Charlene's house in South Louisville.

"I'm sorry I couldn't give you an extravagant honeymoon," Paul said.

"That's okay," Daphne said. "I'm sorry I didn't have my own house."

"After I serve my tour of duty in Iraq, we'll be able to live in many places. Of course, we'll have to live on base, since housing is rent free."

"I'll be happy to be with you—no matter where we live." Daphne kissed Paul.

A month later, Neo drove Paul and Daphne to Fort Knox. Paul was being deployed to Iraq. Paul and Daphne embraced in a kiss before Paul boarded the plane.

Four months later, Daphne attended church with her older cousin, Martha Walter. Martha was known as a troublemaker. After church, Lee Valentine introduced himself to Daphne. Daphne sat on the passenger side of Martha's car.

"I'm Lee Valentine. It's nice to meet you." Lee kissed Daphne's hand.

"She's already married. She's even four months pregnant by her husband," Martha said.

Disappointed, Lee stepped away from the car. Martha then drove off.

Monday evening, Martha brought Lee to Neo and Charlene's house to meet Daphne. Lee wore his army uniform. During dinner, Martha sat Lee next to Daphne. Daphne showed Lee her wedding ring. Lee stared at Daphne the entire time. Neo and Charlene both noticed it. Their three kids—Craig, Monique, and Raheem—also noticed Lee's staring at Daphne.

Saturday afternoon, Lee knocked on the door in his army uniform. Daphne answered.

"I have some bad news for you, Mrs. Williams," Lee said.

"Oh, no." Daphne began to sob.

"Your husband, Private First-Class Paul Williams, died in an explosion." Lee then got into his car and drove off.

Charlene and Monique rushed Daphne to the nearest emergency room.

"The news of your husband's death has put you in jeopardy of having a miscarriage," said Doctor Leonard Payne. "You need to stay at home and rest for a few days."

That evening, Daphne was home alone. Everyone else was at the grocery store. There was a knock at the door. Daphne opened the door, and it was Lee, in civilian clothes.

"Since I gave you the news about your husband, you owe me a date."

"But the doctor said—"

"Don't talk," Lee rudely interrupted. "The Bible says, 'be quick to listen and slow to speak.' In other words, you don't talk."

"Can we wait a few days?"

"No. Go upstairs and put on a pretty dress. We're going on our date tonight."

Daphne went upstairs and put on a pretty dress. She then went on a date with Lee. Lee drove Daphne to Fort Knox so all of his friends could see her. Lee brought Daphne home at five in the morning. Since Daphne was bleeding heavily, Charlene rushed Daphne back to the emergency room. It was too late. Daphne miscarried. She stayed in the hospital for two days.

Friday afternoon, Martha showed up at the house with Lee and Reverend Jesse Valentine, Lee's uncle.

"This is Reverend Valentine, Lee's uncle. Lee wants to marry Daphne, and they plan to get married tomorrow," Martha told Neo and Charlene.

"That's not a good idea," said Neo. "Daphne just lost her husband and had a miscarriage, due to her 'owing' Lee a date."

"Daphne is an extremely beautiful woman," said Jesse. "Lee wants to have her all to himself for the rest of his life. They're getting married tomorrow."

Saturday afternoon, Lee and Daphne got married. They had their honeymoon in Neo and Charlene's basement.

Almost three years later, there was a knock at the door and Neo answered.

"Daphne! A surprise guest is at the door!" shouted Neo.

Question: Who was the surprise guest?

<u>Answer</u>: The surprise guest was Paul. Lee lied about Paul dying in an explosion because he wanted to have Daphne. Lee went to prison for lying. Jesse went to prison for knowingly leading Daphne into polygamy and for holding an illegal wedding ceremony.

The 100-year-old Curse

Libby Creekside was ninety-years-old and being cared for by her great-granddaughters, Bridget and Brenda. Brenda excitedly ran into Libby's bedroom.

"Mama Creekside, we got the ancestry DNA test!" she exclaimed.

Libby had an uneasy expression on her face as Brenda opened the package. Brenda and Bridget both read the results. All three had sad expressions on their faces.

"Papa Creekside wasn't our biological great-grandfather. Mr. James Hartwell was," Bridget said.

"Mama Creekside, you told us you decided to allow Brenda and me have this land after you die. Why would you give this land to us if we're not the biological descendants of Jacob Creekside? Is it because it's cursed?" asked Bridget.

"Every hunting dog Papa Creekside owned died from parvo on this land," said Brenda. "Also, Brenda and I have nightmares about the woods behind this house."

"I was Jacob's second wife, after your biological great-grandmother, Apple, died. He was thirty years older than I was when we got married. Jacob confessed something to me before he died." Libby pointed to a drawer. Bridget opened the drawer and pulled out a journal.

"I must pass his confession on to you," said Libby.

After Libby went to sleep, Bridget and Brenda read the journal.

Flashback

Jacob Creekside, who walked with a limp, stood outside in front of a store which read, *Hartwell's Store for Colored People* on the front door. The owner was Mr. James Hartwell.

"Did you get injured in the war?" James asked Jacob.

"I got injured overseas, in Europe," responded Jacob.

"I retired from the army after serving three years in Paris, France. I then came home and married Apple Wethington."

"That's a unique name for a woman."

"When her mother was pregnant with her, her father always had to come to the store to buy apples. Her mother always craved apples, so they named her Apple when she was born."

"Has this store always been in your family?"

"After slavery, the white Hartwells gave this land and this store to the black Hartwells."

"All of this land is yours?"

"Yes, it is. It's good farmland too. My wife, four sons and two daughters help harvest the land and I sell the food to the local colored folks here."

Three white men stood in front of the store.

"I hear that in Paris, France, you can have all the white women you want!" Jacob shouted to James as he glanced at the three white men.

"Apple's the only woman for me." James grew afraid.

"Are you sure you never gave illegitimate half-breed babies to some white women in Paris, France?" Jacob asked as he limped towards the three white men.

"None of that ever happened." James was terrified.

The three white men gave James hostile stares.

The next morning, Apple found James lynched on a tree in the woods behind their house. That afternoon, the church held his funeral in the *Colored Folks' Cemetery,* near James Hartwell's land.

Apple cried over James' grave as Jacob approached her.

"I know it might be too soon, but I need a wife. I was injured in the war, and I have nothing. Can you please be my wife?"

"You're right. It's too soon," sobbed Apple.

"Ma'am, you got six kids without a father and farmland as well as a store. I can take care of it all for you if you marry me tonight," Jacob said.

Jacob and Apple got married by the colored preacher that night.

Over time, all of Jacob's hunting dogs died due to parvo in the ground. Locusts also attacked their crops. The store went out of business. Apple miscarried all of Jacob's children due to the water on the land suddenly being contaminated with waste from a nearby factory. All six of James and Apple's children enlisted in the army and they never came back.

End of Flashback

"It suddenly makes sense," said Brenda.

After Libby died, Brenda and Bridget got the land. No more parvo, contaminated water, and locust invasions. The land became blessed again.

<u>Question</u>: Why was the land cursed?

<u>Answer</u>: Jacob lied to get James lynched. Jacob wanted James' wife, land, and store. Innocent blood was shed because of a lie.

The Hooded Killer

Mr. Luis Vila worked on a customer's car in his auto shop, *Luis' Neighborhood Auto Repair*. The customer sat in the waiting room, texting as he watched Luis through the waiting room window.

Someone in an oversized black hoodie and a full facemask approached Luis. He then shot Luis in the chest five times. The customer called 911. First responders arrived within five minutes and rushed Luis to the hospital, where he died.

Luis' wife, Salina, rushed to the hospital and the doctors gave her the news. Salina was six months pregnant, and the news of her husband's murder devastated her into a miscarriage.

A month later, Salina was at the cemetery, crying over Luis' grave. Reverend Abraham Valentine approached Salina. Two men in gray hoodies stood in a distance, looking at a grave.

"I know that you just buried your husband, but my nephew, Lee Valentine, needs a wife. You've been running away from Lee for years. You even married Luis to escape Lee. Now that Luis is dead, you can marry Lee," said Abraham.

"I didn't get to attend Luis' funeral because I was in the hospital recovering from a miscarriage," sobbed Salina. "My husband's murder caused me to have a miscarriage."

"Judge Roy McCoy and the twelve jurors found Lee not guilty of your husband's murder. The bullets used didn't match any of my nephew's guns. Also, the suspect wore an oversized hoodie. Lee is tall and muscular, and he never wore oversized clothes."

"I currently have no desire to marry Lee or anyone else. Please leave."

"That's not how you talk to a church leader!" Abraham was furious.

"I'm sorry. Please forgive me."

"You'd better be sorry! You will marry Lee! He needs a wife! According to rumors, your husband's murder was your punishment for marrying him instead of Lee. If you don't marry him, then I pray that tragedies occur in your life!"

"Someone murdered my husband. I had a miscarriage, and the miscarriage was so bad, the doctors had to perform a hysterectomy. How can things get worse?"

"I'll pray that tragedies occur with everyone you love if you don't marry Lee. That's not a threat—that's a promise."

It was Saturday afternoon. Lee and Salina stood in front of a church podium and looked at Abraham. Abraham was so thin, his preacher's robe was slightly oversized.

"I now pronounce you husband and wife," Abraham said. "You may kiss each other."

Lee gladly kissed Salina, but Salina hesitantly kissed him back.

The following Sunday, in church, Abraham stood behind the podium. Again, in a preacher's robe that was slightly oversized.

"Does anyone have a testimony?" Abraham asked into the microphone.

"I have a testimony!" shouted Lee as he stood up. "Yesterday, God blessed me with a beautiful wife named Salina." Lee then sat down.

Six months after the marriage, Lee came home from work and found a devastating scene. With an empty bottle of sleeping pills on the floor, Salina was dead on the couch. A suicide note was on the coffee table. The note read:

I miss Luis. I never wanted to marry Lee. Abraham threated to pray for tragedies to occur with everyone I love if I didn't marry Lee. Luis' murder devastated me into a miscarriage of a beautiful girl that I'll never get to raise. According to rumors, Luis' murder was God punishing me for marrying him instead of Lee. I can no longer live with all of this. May God forgive me.

Abraham conducted Salina's funeral. Abraham stayed behind as others left the cemetery. In a distance, two men in grey hoodies stood in front of a grave.

Abraham angrily looked upward. "I did what I did so my nephew could have a wife! Why did you allow her to commit suicide?"

The two men in grey hoodies approached Abraham and arrested him. They were undercover police officers.

Question: How did the police officers know Abraham was guilty of Luis' murder?

<u>Answer</u>: In the cemetery, Abraham shouted, "I did this so my nephew can have a wife!" Also, the shooter was in an oversized hoodie. Abraham was a slim man who wore oversized clothes.

The Truth in the Tooth

"We're thousands of dollars in debt." Sargent Dennis Bean looked at his bills.

"If you die, I get one million dollars," Jill Bean told Dennis.

"Do you want me to die?" Dennis was upset.

"No. I have an idea. We can place the old Corvette on the side of the road and set it on fire. We'll put your clothes and your watch on a random corpse in the driver's seat. But we must first dig up a corpse from the cemetery."

"We must put my clothes and my watch on the corpse, put the corpse in the driver's seat, and fasten the seatbelt before setting it on fire."

"The body will be badly burned and beyond recognition. I stole the driver's license of my late uncle, Julius McCoy. You can use this as your new identity, since Uncle Julius has been dead for six months." Jill handed the driver's license to Dennis.

"I was in the army for over twenty years, and I want out. Faking my death can be my way out." Dennis rubbed his shaved hair and shaved face.

"Fort Knox is surrounded by acres of open land and miles of lonesome roads."

"We're doing this tonight. You'll get your one million dollars. We're going to a nearby cemetery and dig up a recently buried corpse."

"I hope the corpse is near the entrance. I'm scared of cemeteries at night." Jill was nervous.

"According to the obituaries, a ninety-six-year-old woman named Harriet King was buried this afternoon. Hopefully, her grave is near the entrance."

That night, Dennis and Jill arrived at the cemetery wearing black clothes, shoes, and hoodies. Dennis drove the Corvette and Jill drove their SUV. After digging up Harriet's corpse, he placed her in the trunk of the Corvette. There was also a pile of Dennis' dirty clothes in the trunk. Jill used the shovel to replace the dirt.

Dennis and Jill drove down a dark, lonesome road near South Louisville. They stopped beside the road. Dennis pulled the Corvette into a ditch. He took Harriet's corpse out of the trunk, undressed her, and put his dirty clothes on her. He then placed her in the driver's seat, fastened the seatbelt, and placed his watch on Harriet's wrist. Afterwards, he forcefully pulled a tooth from her mouth, and put it into his pants pocket.

Dennis pulled a match from his pocket, lit it, and put it into the gas tank. Afterwards, Dennis quickly jumped into the SUV, and Jill sped away.

Saturday morning, Dennis and Jill watched the news.

"This is Shannon Choi, with your Saturday morning news. Today, firefighters put out a car fire near South Louisville. The body in the car was burned beyond recognition. The Police Department in South Louisville and the Military Police in Fort Knox are investigating..."

Dennis and Jill gave each other a high-five.

Sunday morning, James Reeves and Tito Rodriguez, two MPs, knocked on the Beans' door. Jill answered. "Is this about my husband?!" She pretended to be upset.

"Your husband's car was found on fire yesterday," James told Jill.

Jill allowed the MPs in. She then handed James the tooth, which was in a sandwich bag.

"I'm Julius McCoy, Jill's uncle, is this regarding my nephew-in-law?" Dennis, in disguise, pretended to be concerned. He wore a long, blond wig and a blond goatee.

The following Friday, Dennis and Jill were arrested for fraud.

"I gave you Dennis' extracted tooth from his last dental appointment. That tooth should match the person in the burnt Corvette." Jill was upset.

"The tooth belonged to an old, black woman. Dennis is a middle-aged white man," Tito said as he arrested Jill.

"I'll bet you wished you'd learned Forensic Odontology while in the army," James told Dennis as he arrested him.

Question: How did the MPs find out who the tooth belonged to?

_____

<u>Answer</u>: A forensic dentist can extract DNA from the pulp chamber and use it for identification. Teeth have a very rich source of DNA. Forensic odontologists can determine the gender, race, and age (at the time of death) of the person the tooth came from.

Their Beauty

Henry Tonnarelli and Richard Stamos were restaurant owners who moved to Poetstown, Kentucky because they wanted to live in a beautiful, small city.

"Poetstown, Kentucky was nominated *Most Beautiful Small City in America* once every decade. In the past, Poetstown was filled with acres of open fields. Children spent hours playing in the open fields during summer vacation. In the past decade, whiskey franchisers have built distilleries in these open fields," said Henry.

"A vodka franchiser from Russia also built a vodka distillery in Poetstown. His family and he visited Poetstown and fell in love with the town's beauty. The vodka franchiser and his family then moved here," Richard added.

"My family and I moved here and brought our Italian restaurant franchise with us, from Brooklyn, New York. We created many jobs for the residents here."

"My family and I brought our Greek restaurant franchise from Athens, New York. We, too, chose to live here because of this small city's beauty. My grandparents visited Poetstown from Greece, and they now want to move here."

"Other business owners come here and want to exploit this beautiful city," Henry said as he looked at the acres of distilleries.

"Just like some people exploit beautiful women, there are those who like to exploit beautiful cities. It's an eye sore to look at acres of whiskey distilleries."

"Our families came to bring job creation with food—not liquor. Farmers in surrounding farm towns grow our produce, and we pay them a fair salary."

"To have some distilleries is fine. There are now distilleries in every area that used to be open land. Too many business owners are coming here and building distilleries. This beautiful city is slowly being destroyed with acres of distilleries."

"Beautiful women and beautiful cities both have one thing in common," said Henry.

"I already know what it is," responded Richard.

"There was a movie about a king who went to prophets in a high mountain to seek counsel about an upcoming war. These prophets had a beautiful priestess dance for the king. One of the prophets then made a comment about a woman and her beauty."

"I know exactly which movie you're talking about. The saying about a woman's beauty is centuries old. The same saying also pertains to beautiful places. Many people want to visit and live in beautiful places. These beautiful places then become overpopulated."

"When we first moved here, there were only two high schools. They now must build a third one. I hope the mayor of Poetstown decides to tear down the old, abandoned drive-in, and build the third high school there."

"I also hope the group of old, abandoned distilleries on Heaven Hill can be torn down and become another middle school."

"This city is filled with young, beautiful women and I'm concerned about businessmen coming here to exploit them. We already have men from Fort Knox coming here every weekend."

"You and I need to work together to be sure nobody exploits our female relatives. Let's promise to look out for each other's female relatives," Richard said.

"It's a deal," Henry agreed. "I promise to watch over your female relatives as well as mine."

Henry and Richard shook hands.

"No wonder the men here keep their shotguns loaded." Richard laughed. "They have their beautiful daughters, sisters, nieces, and cousins to protect."

"We learned from them and keep loaded shotguns nearby," Henry agreed.

"I wish there were ways to prevent so many businesspeople from coming here and buying up land. There was a time when only tourists came to Poetstown. They spent their money and then left."

"Richard, your family and you are from Athens, New York. My family and I are from Brooklyn, New York. Both of our families moved here from somewhere else."

"We moved here to establish restaurant businesses and create jobs. Neither of us moved here to bring acres of distilleries."

"You do have a point there."

"Like I said before, beautiful women and beautiful cities both have one thing in common."

"We both know what it is." Henry sighed.

Question: What do beautiful women and cities both have in common?

_____

<u>Answer</u>: Their beauty is also their curse.

Tire Slashers

"Out of all the truck stops we've been to, I love returning to Waddy!" Roy McCoy pulled his semi into the truck stop in Waddy, Kentucky.

To the side of the truck stop, was a billboard advertising *Tony's Tire World*.

"That tire place is new." Roy looked up at the billboard. "That wasn't here last year."

"What's the name of that place?" Louise McCoy, Roy's wife, asked.

The billboard says *Tony's Tire World*."

"I'll Google the information about them on my phone." Louise started her search. "It's been in Waddy for only ten months. They do a lot of business. Also, they accept most insurances if your tires get slashed or something."

"From what I hear, Waddy has very little crime. The last time somebody tried to rob the Waddy truck stop, he was jumped from behind and beaten up. The young man tried to rob them using a knife."

"I also know that many people around here have shotguns. Nobody wants to try anything with anybody around here."

Roy pulled into the truck stop and fueled up. Afterwards, Roy and Louise got something to eat. Roy took a shower in the men's shower area, while Louise took one in the ladies'. After their showers, they climbed back into the truck and went to sleep.

The next morning, Roy and Louise climbed out of the truck and went inside the truck stop to eat breakfast. When they came back out, they discovered that all eighteen wheels on their semi were slashed.

"This happened again?" Brenda Calbert came out of the truck stop, very upset. "This has been happening to truckers for the past ten months!"

"What do you mean 'for the past ten months?'" Louise asked.

"Every week, for the past ten months, truckers' tires get slashed. The good news is Tony Peach tows the semis to his business for free. Also, the truckers' companies pay for the replacement of the tires." Brenda had a frustrated tone in her voice.

"You work third shift here. Don't you ever see anything?"
Louise was furious.

"I'm so busy helping customers that I can't stand at the window and guard customers' trucks. Even at midnight, this truck stop stays really busy."

In front of the truck stop, was the billboard advertising *Tony's Tire World*.

"I'm going to call *Tony's Tire World*." Roy dialed the number on the billboard.

Frank Peach came out with the tow truck.

"I'm Frank Peach, and Tony's my father. I'm going to tow your semi to *Tony's Tire World* which is only a block from this truck stop. Would you two like to ride along?"

"Yes. Thank you." Roy helped Louise into the middle of the front seat of the tow truck. Roy then climbed into the passenger seat.

By noon, all eighteen tires were replaced.

"The *James Trucking Company* sent me eighteen thousand dollars through Cash App. And I'm so sorry this happened." Frank handed Roy the receipt.

"We're six hours late getting our cargo down to Nashville, Tennessee. Thank you for everything." Roy shook hands with Frank.

Louise also shook hands with Frank, then she and Roy got into the semi and drove off.

It was Saturday night, and Brenda arrived at the truck stop at ten o'clock. Video cameras were installed throughout the parking lot. They were on the same poles as the streetlights. There were also signs which read, *Warning! These premises are being videotaped twenty-four hours a day.*

"I'm here to give you your thirty-minute break," Brett Howley, Brenda's boss, told her.

Brenda brought breakfast to her husband, Jamal. Jamal worked in the camera room.

"Thank you for getting me this job." Jamal spoke between bites.

"It's about time they installed cameras and hired somebody to guard the parking lot. You've been in the army for twenty years, and you used to guard the posts." Brenda also spoke between bites.

Jamal and Brenda both looked into a camera and saw two people, wearing black hoodies and holding ice picks, walking towards a truck. Jamal immediately called the police.

Question: Who were the tire slashers?

_____

<u>Answer</u>: The tire slashers were Tony Peach and his son, Frank. They were both arrested and put in jail. They also lost their business.

True Beauty

Marsha Lewis and Gina Pendleton showed up at East Side Park at the same time.

"We're going to settle this once and for all about who's the most beautiful lady in Kentville!" said Marsha.

"I'm the most beautiful lady in Kentville! I have longer hair, and my fur lashes are more expensive than yours!" Gina batted her eyes and shook her hair extensions around.

"I got my nose and lips done by the best plastic surgeon in Kentville! I also bought the best air-brushed foundation on the market."

All the single guys in the park gathered around Marsha and Gina. Among them, were two brothers named Jacob and Jordan Wells.

Zora Ellis drove into the park with her six-year-old nephew, Coy Ellis, sitting in his booster seat in the back. All the guys in the park, including Jacob and Jordan, watched Zora and Coy get out of the car. Zora held Coy's hand as they entered the park.

They watched Zora as she played with Coy. Zora pushed Coy on the swing set. She then pushed him on the merry-go-round. Afterwards, she went down the sliding board with Coy multiple times. Zora and Coy had so much fun.

Marsha and Gina stopped arguing and looked at all the guys.

"Why are all of you looking at Zora? She wears t-shirts, bike shorts, and canvas shoes! She doesn't wear high-cost clothes and shoes like me!" shouted Marsha.

"Look at her face! She has freckles on her face, and she has a funny-shaped nose. She also has braces on her teeth. She doesn't have a flawless face and perfect, straight teeth like I do!" shouted Gina.

"She also has shoulder-length, curly hair and she doesn't have long, flowing hair that blows in the wind like mine," Marsha shook her long hair extensions around again.

"Look at her short, manicured fingernails. I get my nails done at the nail salon every Saturday morning. I have long, beautiful nails!" Gina showed off her acrylic nails.

"I have long fingernails, too! I also have expensive fur lashes." Marsha batted her eyes and showed off her long, acrylic nails.

"To us, Zora is the most beautiful lady in East Side Park," Jordan told Marsha and Gina.

"I agree," said Jacob.

Coy approached Marsha and Gina.

"My aunt is the most beautiful girl in the park!" Coy told Marsha and Gina.

"It sounds like three to zero to us," Jordan told Marsha and Gina.

Jacob and Jordan each gave Coy the fist-bump.

All the other guys in East Side Park nodded their heads in agreement.

"Come on, Coy," Zora told the boy. "We're about to go home so I can fix your lunch. We can then watch your favorite movies."

Zora put Coy into his booster seat. She then got into her car, put on her seatbelt, and drove away. All the single guys in the park watched as she left.

"We're going to West Side Park, and we'll let the single guys there determine which one of us is the most beautiful lady in Kentville!" shouted Marsha.

"The guys in East Side Park have bad taste!" said Gina. "They think that Zora Ellis is beautiful. They, apparently, don't have standards when it comes to looks."

"Bye!" shouted Jordan.

"We're not going to miss you!" Jacob yelled.

Marsha got into her yellow convertible and drove off.

Gina got into her red convertible and drove off.

Marsha and Gina stood in the middle of West Side Park.

"Who's the most beautiful lady in Kentville?" Marsha shouted to all the guys in the park.

"I have longer, prettier hair!" shouted Gina. "I also have longer, prettier acrylic nails."

All the guys in West Side Park walked away from Marsha and Gina.

"Zora is the most beautiful lady in Kentville!" shouted a guy in the crowd.

"Why is that?" asked Marsha. "That makes no sense!"

Marsha and Gina angrily stormed out of West Side Park.

Question: Why did all the single guys consider Zora the most beautiful lady in Kentville?

_____

<u>Answer</u>: Marsha and Gina both had artificial and "bought" beauty. Zora had both inner beauty and outer natural beauty. Zora had true beauty.

Victim Blame

Mrs. Jazmine Bivins, a rich widow, was in court with Tyrone Stoner, a career criminal. Jazmine's lawyer was Attorney John Choi. Tyrone's was Attorney Newt Lynch, the best criminal attorney in the city.

Attorney Choi stood in front of the twelve jurors. "This is the gun that Tyrone Stoner used to shoot open Jazmine's safe. He then stole her bank card and bank account information and gave the information to his girlfriend, Angela Adamson." Attorney Choi showed the jurors the gun.

The jurors gave Tyrone judgmental stares as Attorney Choi sat down.

Attorney Lynch then stood in front of the jurors. "We're aware of Tyrone's criminal background. But Jazmine is at fault. Although the safe is fireproof, there's a defect with the safe. This defect makes all this Jazmine's fault. This defect made it easy for a career criminal, like Tyrone, to get into the safe," the defense attorney said.

The jurors whispered among each other.

Attorney Lynch called Jazmine to the witness stand. Jazmine came forward.

"Mrs. Jazmine Bivins, first of all, my condolences on your loss," said Attorney Lynch.

"Thank you so much. It's been almost a year since Berry's death, but I'm still grieving."

"I also give my condolences," Judge Troy Brown told Jazmine.

"Thank you so much, Judge Brown," Jazmine sadly responded.

"When you first allowed Angela Adamson and her children to live in your house, were you aware that her boyfriend, Tyrone Stoner, was a career criminal?" asked Attorney Lynch.

"Yes," sobbed Jazmine.

"If you were aware that Angela Adamson had children with a career criminal, then why did you allow them to live in your house?"

"My preacher, Reverend Jerome Weaver, persuaded me to. Something about Jesus saying, 'Give to the poor' and how it's my obligation to give Angela and her children a place to live and provide for them, since I'm a rich widow."

"By allowing the mother of his children in your house, you invited this kind of criminal activity into your home and into your life."

All twelve jurors gave Jazmine judgmental stares.

"Are you aware that your late husband's fireproof safe had a specific defect?"

"I wasn't aware of this defect until after the incident occurred."

"I never asked you when you became aware. I asked you if you were aware. Are you aware of the specific defect with the safe?"

"Yes."

"The specific defect with the safe is why Tyrone was able to shoot it open. You made it easy for a career criminal to shoot open the safe. He then stole your bank card and your bank account information and gave them to Angela."

"Objection!" shouted Attorney Choi.

"On what grounds?" asked Judge Brown.

"Before Tyrone shot open the safe, he beat up Jazmine and threw her out of her house. She was living with her sister-in-law, Wanda, when Tyrone did this," Attorney Choi argued.

"This isn't about where Jazmine was when this incident occurred. This is about the specific defect that made the safe easy for Tyrone to shoot it open," argued Attorney Lynch.

"Attorney Lynch is right," Judge Brown told Attorney Choi. "This is about the specific defect which allowed Tyrone to shoot open the safe and steal Jazmine's card and bank information."

Attorney Choi sat down reluctantly.

"All of us agree on the defect about the safe?" Attorney Lynch stood in front of the jury.

The jurors whispered among themselves again.

Soon after, they left the courtroom to make a decision and came out five minutes later with their verdict.

"Has the jury reached a verdict?" Judge Brown asked.

The first juror stoop up. "In the case of theft and property destruction, we, the jury, find Mr. Tyrone Stoner not guilty. In the case of physical assault, we, the jury, find Mr. Tyrone Stoner guilty."

Judge Brown looked at Tyrone. "Mr. Tyrone Stoner, you have been found guilty of physical assault." Next, he glanced at two guards and said., "Guards, take him away!"

Jazmine cheered as the guards handcuffed Tyrone and escorted him out of the courtroom.

Question: What was the specific defect with the safe?

<u>Answer</u>: The safe was not bullet-proof.

What the Mortician Knew

Crystal Brady sat in Attorney Ron Weaver's office at *The Law Office of Lynch and Weaver*.

"Ron, I have four kids by your nephew, Andre. Please tell him to do his internship with Mr. Edward Preston so he can become a mortician and marry me," Crystal begged Ron.

"Why would I do that?" Ron asked. "You're on government assistance."

"Kentucky has a temporary form of government assistance called *Temporary Assistance for Families in Need*. It's also known as *TAFFIN*. I'm about to get my *TAFFIN* terminated soon."

"Andre doesn't want to get married until he turns fifty. Until then, he wants to enjoy life and the ladies a little longer. You need to find another man to marry you and raise your kids. Robert Keeps recently inherited ten-million dollars from his late great-grandfather."

"He married Zara six months ago."

"That's tragic." Ron pulled a gun out of his desk and handed it to Crystal.

"What do I do with this?" Crystal asked as she took the gun.

"Lure her to the waterfront after midnight. Afterwards, shoot her, execution style, and throw her into the river." Ron reclined. "Problem solved."

"I'll call her and tell her that my date beat me up and left me at the waterfront." Crystal put the gun into her purse.

The following morning, Zara was found floating in the river. Two police scuba divers got her corpse out of the river.

Edward Preston, the mortician, put her into a body bag, zipped it up, and loaded it into the back of his SUV.

At the morgue, Edward did a full autopsy on Zara and documented everything he found.

Attorney Newt Lynch represented Crystal in court.

"Zara committed suicide and jumped into the river. She was miserable in her marriage," Attorney Lynch told the twelve jurors. He then sat down.

Attorney Ming Li, Robert Keeps' attorney, stood up in front of the twelve jurors.

"Zara was murdered, execution style, and her dead body was thrown into the river. Mr. Edward Preston, the best mortician in the city, will testify to that. According to his autopsy report, Zara was dead before she ended up in the river," Attorney Li told the twelve jurors. He then sat down.

"Mr. Edward Preston, approach the witness stand," Judge Troy Brown told Edward.

Edward was sworn in before he sat down.

"Do you have proof that Zara was dead before she was in the river? Do you have proof that she didn't drown?" Attorney Lynch asked.

"Yes, I do." Edward pulled out an autopsy report and handed it to Attorney Lynch.

"This proves nothing." Attorney Lynch glanced over the report. "I consider this report as insufficient evidence."

"I'll be the judge of that." Judge Brown took the autopsy report from Newt and read it. "Have all twelve jurors view the evidence." Judge Brown handed the autopsy report to the security guard.

The security guard passed the autopsy report to the jury.

All twelve jurors nodded in agreement.

"A silly autopsy report proves nothing!" Attorney Lynch was nervous. "Zara shot herself in the back of the head, survived, and then jumped into the river."

"It was impossible for Zara to shoot herself in the back of the head," Attorney Li said. "She was shot execution style."

Thirty minutes after the jury went into seclusion, they returned with a verdict.

"Has the jury reached a verdict?" Judge Brown asked the first juror.

The first juror stood up. "We find Ms. Crystal Brady guilty of murder in the first degree."

"Ms. Crystal Brady, you'll spend twenty years to life in the Women's Correctional Center in Pewee Valley, Kentucky." Judge Brown pounded his gavel as the guards handcuffed her and escorted her out of the courtroom. "Court is adjourned."

"I'm aware that she couldn't shoot herself in the back of the head. But how did you know that she didn't drown in the river?" Attorney Lynch asked Edward.

"Read the autopsy report again." Edward handed it to the lawyer to read again.

Question: How did Edward know that Zara didn't drown?

<u>Answer</u>: According to the autopsy report, there was no water in Zara's lungs. Once a person dies, they stop breathing.

What was in the Attic?

Keith Ellington decided to open his huge vintage home to Edward Wells and his family.

"Since you are a widower like me, I'm only going to charge you six-hundred dollars a month. I also ask that you go half on the landline phone and utility bills," Keith told Edward.

"Thank you for allowing me, my goddaughter, my granddaughter, and my grandson-in-law to stay here. Not everyone would do that," Edward said gratefully.

"My wife died of cancer two years ago, and all six of our children are in the military. It gets very lonely in this huge house."

Edward looked up at the attic. "What's in the attic?"

"Don't go into the attic, and don't ask about it," Keith answered.

Edward gave Keith the rent money, and Keith put it into his wallet. Keith then left the house and drove away in his SUV.

Edward and his family all stood in the hallway and stared up at the attic with curiosity.

Every night, Keith went up into the attic and brought down large bags of items. He then took them out to the detached garage in the backyard. Early in the morning, he loaded up the items into the back of his SUV and drove away. Keith came home in the afternoon and slept for the rest of the day. This continued every night throughout most of December.

Some neighbors, who came in from their second shift jobs, saw Keith working in the garage. Others, who left for the third shift jobs, also saw Keith working in the garage. When they came in from their third shift jobs, they saw Keith load bags of items into his SUV. The neighbors who left for their first shift jobs witnessed Keith loading bags of items into his SUV. They all wondered what he was up to.

Multiple neighbors called the city's anonymous police tip line about Keith. Undercover police officers began to watch him throughout the night. James Reeves, an undercover police officer, followed Keith every morning. Keith went to a shelter in the downtown area and dropped off bags of items.

It was early morning on Christmas Eve. Keith stayed at the shelter to help all the volunteers with the Christmas presents. They put gifts into shiny Christmas bags and put names of shelter residents on the shiny Christmas bags.

Officers from the city's police department barged into the shelter. Keith and all the other volunteers were startled!

"According to anonymous tips, Keith Ellington is involved in suspicious activities," shouted Officer Reeves.

"None of these items were stolen," Keith pleaded.

"Do you have receipts to prove you didn't steal them?" asked Officer Reeves.

"I never kept any receipts. All these items are vintage," responded Keith.

"Why would you give old stuff to anybody? Are shelter home recipients not good enough for store bought stuff?"

Joseph Stevens intervened. "Officer, I'm Joseph Stevens, the shelter director. These residents lost everything in house fires or floods or evictions or lawsuits. They're grateful for whatever they receive. They're not picky."

"Officer, my wife died of cancer two years ago, and even before she died, she asked that I get rid of all our surplus stuff. I've always been a hoarder," Keith explained.

"Where do you live?" Officer Reeves inquired.

"Follow me to my house," Keith replied.

Officer Reeves and other police officers followed Keith to his house.

Edward and his family grew nervous when they saw all the police cars following Keith home.

"I hope this isn't because of my expired tags," said Dallas Hicks, Edward's grandson-in-law.

"Did someone snitch on me because I ran a red light last week?" asked Mia Meadows, Edward's goddaughter.

"I bought the boys' toys from a garage sale last week. I hope the toys were not stolen," McKenna, Edward's granddaughter, said.

All the police officers followed Keith into the house.

"Show us your attic!" shouted Officer Reeves.

Question: What was in the attic?

<u>Answer</u>: The attic was full of items that once belonged to Keith and his family. Everyone spent all of Christmas Eve cleaning and putting items into gift bags to donate to the shelter home residents. Merry Christmas!

How did a Blessing Become a Curse?

Robert Keeps just married Zara. Zara became Mrs. Zara (Ellington) Keeps. Both the Ellington and Keeps families celebrated their unity. The only people unhappy with the wedding were Reverend Andrew Weaver and his family.

Reverend Weaver had a "talk" with Reverend Abraham Bingham in Reverend Weaver's office on the following Monday.

"Why did you allow Robert to marry Zara when there are poor, single mothers who need rich husbands?" Reverend Weaver was furious. "Robert inherited ten-million from his late great-grandfather, Thurston Wethington, for getting married before his thirtieth birthday!"

"You know you're looking for somebody to marry your niece, Crystal. She has two children and twins on the way by Andre Milton," responded Reverend Bingham.

"Zara's rich! She doesn't need a husband! Her maternal grandmother established the *Berries of Sweden* hair care empire, and her maternal grandfather established the *Flowers of Sweden* perfume empire. When her grandparents die, Zara, her sister, Zoe, and their cousins get all that money. Zara's nothing but a selfish gold digger, anyway."

"Somebody needs to make Andre man up and get a job so he can support his children. Besides, none of Crystal's children belong to Robert. He never even touched Crystal."

"All the jails are overcrowded, and police are overworked. Nobody can make Andre get a job to pay his child-support." Reverend Weaver spoke in a frustrated tone.

"This conversation is over. Robert and Zara are married, and that's final!" Reverend Bingham got up. "Have a good day," he said as he left the office.

Reverend Bingham sat in front of his TV and watched the Monday night news.

"This is Shannon Choi and I'm reporting from the cliff where Mrs. Zara Keeps was thrown off. Andre Milton was taken into custody. Andre will be defended by Attorney Newt Lynch, the best criminal attorney in the state."

Attorney Lynch spoke next. "What was done, was done for children. Crystal and her children live in a dangerous neighborhood. For Crystal, a rich husband is her only ticket out of poverty, and a rich stepfather is her children's only way out of a dangerous neighborhood."

"According to my sources, none of Crystal's children belong to Robert Keeps. All her children belong to Andre Milton," Shannon said.

"Zara was a selfish and greedy gold digger. She even got pregnant by Robert two months ago to trap him into marriage," said Attorney Lynch.

The following Monday was the trial.

Shannon Choi stood in front of the courthouse reporting the news. "Andre Milton was acquitted on all charges. All twelve jurors agreed that what was done was done so Crystal can have the husband she needs and her poor, deprived children can have the rich stepfather they need."

Tuesday morning, Robert stood over Zara's grave and cried.

Reverend Weaver approached Robert. "My condolences."

Robert angrily remained silent.

"I'm sorry for what happened to Zara, but Crystal is in desperate need of a husband. She's about to get her government assistance terminated to the state's five-year-limit law. You're the richest man in the city," said Reverend Weaver.

"No!" shouted Robert.

"I still remember your confessions to me from your days in business college."

Robert looked horrified.

"You went to bed with some female instructors so you could graduate from business college at the top of your class. I know you don't want your secret to be exposed."

The following Saturday, Robert married Crystal in the church. Reverend Weasel officiated.

The following Sunday, Mother Oliver, the oldest woman in church, approached Crystal.

"You may not realize this, but a blessing can also become a curse," Mother Oliver told her.

"That makes no sense! I got a rich husband, and that's a blessing. My kids got a rich stepfather, and that's a blessing. I don't have to listen to you!" Crystal shouted.

A week after Robert married Crystal, a sniper shot at Crystal and her children. Zoe, Zara's sister, was eventually arrested for being the sniper.

Question: How did a blessing become a curse?

<u>Answer</u>: Robert's inheritance was considered a "financial" blessing. Zara was murdered so Robert could marry Crystal. Zoe shot at Crystal and her children for revenge.

Where was the Money Hidden?

Jessica Creek, an eighty-five-year-old widow, read a journal left by her great-grandfather, Ned Wells. Jessica read the journal to four of her great-grandchildren, Brenda, Francine, Frank, and Joseph. They all sat around the fireplace in her big farmhouse in Bloomfield.

"A group of outlaws called the Quantrill Raiders came through Kentucky in the 1880s. Another outlaw robbed a bank in Russellville, Kentucky in broad daylight. There's a plaque posted in front of the bank in Russellville about the famous robbery. The outlaws buried the treasure somewhere between Bloomfield and Taylorsville. The outlaws hid in a barn in Wakefield for a week," Jessica began to read.

"Where did they bury the treasure?" asked Brenda.

"That's a mystery," answered Jessica. "People have been searching for the money for over a hundred years. In the 1980s, the army came in from Fort Knox with metal detectors, looking for the chest filled with money. When my great-granddad, Ned, was a little boy, he saw a group of men with lanterns by a tree, in the middle of the night." Jessica pointed outside. "That two-hundred-year-old elm tree outside this window." The hollow area in the tree faced the house.

"Do you think they buried it next to the tree?" Joseph asked.

"According to my great-granddad's journal, it was very dark outside, and he couldn't see exactly what they were doing. As a small child, he assumed all the men had to pee at the same time." Jessica chuckled.

All four of the children laughed too.

"People have checked the ground around that tree for decades. People even dug up the ground as far as ten miles around this land. Nothing," Jessica told them.

"Do you think they loaded everything onto a wagon, and they took it with them to Missouri?" Francine asked.

"In our history class, we're learning about the Quantrill Raiders who came through here," Frank, Francine's twin brother, said. "All the outlaws were either caught by lawmen, or they fled to other states and never returned to Kentucky."

"The barn the Quantrill Raiders hid in has been gone for years. But the plaque in front of where the barn used to be stands where the Quantrill Raiders hid. The Quantrill Raiders' story is the only thing that made this area temporarily famous," Jessica informed them.

It began to get windy outside. All the children's mobile phones sent alerts. Jessica's turned on the radio, which announced an alert.

"Get to a basement or another safe location immediately! Heavy winds are coming through both Nelson and Spencer Counties," warned the weather announcer.

The mobile phones read, "Alert! Heavy winds coming through Nelson and Spencer Counties! Get to a lower level if you can! If you can't, then get to a room with no windows!"

All the children helped their great-grandmother get down to the basement by putting her into her stairlift. Joseph then pushed the button downward.

All five stayed in the basement overnight. The basement had all the necessary accommodations, such as a bathroom and a dorm-sized refrigerator filled with food and beverages. There was also a sectional couch and a sofa bed so everyone could sleep.

The next day, everyone went outside and saw that the wind had blown down the two-hundred-year-old elm tree. The wind pushed the tree out by the roots. The tree landed on the hill next to the house, and the winds didn't damage the house. The tree was sideways, and the hollow part continued to face the house. Something had fallen out of the hollow part of the tree.

"We now know why nobody was able to find the treasure chest filled with money. Even with metal detectors," Brenda said.

All five of them looked at the hollow part of the tree in amazement.

Question: What fell out of the hollow part of the tree?

Answer: The treasure chest filled with money fell out of the hollow part of the old elm tree. All four of Jessica's great-grandchildren drove to Russellville and returned the money to the bank. All those searching for the treasure had looked in the ground, but nobody thought to look in the tree.

Who Snitched?

Pastor Floyd Muse clicked the red intercom button, which reached the people outside.

"Deacon James Haydon, please come to my office!"

James came back into the building, went into the church office, and shut the door.

"You did a wonderful sermon on marriage today," James complimented Floyd. "The congregation was confused about how some women must do something in order to be worthy of marriage and worthy of you in marriage."

"I wasn't going to marry Zara Ellington, anyway!" Floyd shouted.

"What's wrong with Zara?" James asked. "She's a beautiful woman, from a very wealthy Swedish-American family."

"She's half-Swedish. Her father is American. Her father met and married her mother while he was stationed at Bowden Army Air Base in Sweden. I don't care about her family establishing the *Flowers of Sweden* perfume, and the *Berries of Sweden* hair products empires!"

"She did everything to win your love," James said. "She even sold the business of her late husband, Paul Ellington, and gave the money to poor parents here in Alexburg."

"I never planned to marry Zara. I married Anna McCoy. I just pretended to want Zara as a way to get her to give her late husband's entire fortune to poor, struggling parents in our community. How else were they going to get free money?"

"That sounds like extortion to me."

"I'll be happy to confess everything to you." Floyd picked up his Bible. "Besides, the Bible says that confession is good for the soul. We're both in this office alone. Why not?"

"Don't you think you need to close the window first?" James glanced at the open window.

Floyd went to the window. He stuck his head outside and looked around. He then shut the window. While Floyd did that, James double-clicked the red intercom button.

Floyd quickly turned around and saw James.

"I saw what you did," Floyd responded. He walked to the desk and pushed the red button.

James looked nervous.

"Now, for my confession." Floyd reclined in his chair. "I just deceived Zara and her family into believing that I wanted to marry her. I then secretly told her that in order to have me as a husband, then she must use all her late husband's money to help poor people in Alexburg."

"Is that why she sold her late husband's company and used the money to make the court-ordered child-support payments for all the deadbeat parents in Alexburg? She even made payments for those who were incarcerated for non-support."

"Because of me, non-compliant parents are out of jail or prison. Also, poor parents were given the money they needed to support their children. Because of me, poor parents got the money they needed to support their children. I made life better for poor people."

"Zara married Robert Keeps, the man she sold Paul's company to. She's now pregnant with her first child—a girl."

"I'm so happy for her." Floyd sarcastically clapped.

"Due to your persuading Zara to sell Paul's company and use the money to pay deadbeat parents' child-support payments, Zara's family no longer trusts her. If they die, then the companies will be given to Zara's younger sister, Zoe, and her younger brother, Logan. Zara gets nothing although she's the oldest."

"Zara's parents were so desperate for her to remarry, and I used the situation to my advantage. Paul and she never had children. They hoped Zara's next husband would give them grandchildren."

"By not marrying Zara, were you punishing her for coming from a wealthy family?"

"Yes. You grew up poor, like I did. I've always been prejudiced towards wealthy people. I'm sure you have too."

"I never was," James answered.

Floyd got up, grabbed his car keys, and left the office. James followed behind him.

Out in the parking lot, all the congregation members gave Floyd hostile stares. Police officers waited in the parking lot, and they handcuffed Floyd.

"Who snitched on me?" Floyd yelled to the crowd.

Question: Who snitched on Floyd?

<u>Answer</u>: Floyd snitched on himself. When James double clicked the intercom button, the first time turned it on, and the second time turned it off. Floyd never realized he turned the intercom back on.

Who Was the Shooter?

Officer James Reeves was called to the Derby Estates Housing Division regarding a window peeper. Peter Johnson, a fifteen-year-old boy, was peeking into the bedroom window of Jill Spratt, the seventeen-year-old niece of News Reporter Kevin Walton. Officer Reeves stood to Peter's left. Peter was shot!

Officer Reeves, a witness to the shooting, called 911. An ambulance arrived immediately.

The following morning, Kevin did the news report.

"I'm Kevin Walton, reporting from the scene of last night's shooting. A fifteen-year-old boy named Peter Johnson was shot while walking home from the house of Jill Spratt, his girlfriend. According to witnesses, Officer James Reeves was the shooter."

Officer Reeves sat in front of his TV, horrified.

"Although Officer Reeves was the person to call 911, he did that as a cover-up. The officer assumed that Peter was peeking in Jill Spratt's bedroom window and shot him.

Officer Reeves is on suspension until the investigation is over. I hope he serves prison time," Kevin reported while he stood in front of news cameras.

Other police officers and reporters were at the shooting scene.

"That's a nice revolver," Officer Candida Rodriguez told Kevin.

"It's a Smith & Wesson 642. You can never be too safe," Kevin proudly responded. "Also, this is easy to draw without snagging."

"It's a beauty," said Officer Rodriguez.

"Thank you." Kevin showed it to the others.

"Peter Johnson is not my boyfriend!" shouted Jill, as Shannon Choi, another news reporter, interviewed her. "I never knew he was peeking in my window while I slept until last night."

"You never called the police?" Shannon Choi asked Jill.

"No!" Jill was really upset. "I pray and hope that Peter survives. In fact, my entire family and church family are all praying for him."

"Do you have an idea of who did the shooting?" Shannon asked Jill.

"I was asleep when I was awakened by gunshots. I'm not a witness to who did the shooting. All the residents were asleep until we were awakened by the sound of the gunshots. Kevin Walton is my uncle, and I don't know why he calls Peter my boyfriend," Jill said as she looked into the camera.

That following night, Shannon stood in front of Children's Hospital.

"Peter Johnson has survived the shooting. He was shot in the right arm, and he is expected to fully recover," Shannon reported. "The bullet removed from Peter's arm came from a specific type of revolver."

Officer Reeves sighed in relief as he watched TV in his living room. He then pulled out his single-shot pistol and was confused. He made phone calls to Officer Rodriguez, Shannon Choi, and his attorney, Troy Brown.

Attorney Brown visited all the gun shops near Derby Estates Housing Division. Troy hand-delivered gun purchase documents of Officer Reeves to both Officer Rodriguez and Shannon Choi. He kept a copy for himself.

Peter was returning home from the hospital as Kevin and Shannon were there to interview him for the news stations.

"Do you forgive Officer Reeves for shooting you?" Kevin asked Peter.

"I don't know who shot me," Peter replied. "It was dark outside."

"Do you know something we don't know?" Mrs. Julie Johnson, Peter's mother, asked Kevin.

Officer Reeves, Officer Rodriguez, and Attorney Brown arrived at the Johnsons' house.

"You have a lot of nerve being here," Kevin told Officer Reeves. "You shoot Peter, and then you come here to welcome him home?"

The Johnsons gave Officer Reeves hostile stares.

Officer Rodriguez then handcuffed Kevin.

"What's this all about?" yelled Kevin.

"You're being arrested for attempted murder," Officer Rodriguez told Kevin. "You have the right to remain silent…" the officer read Kevin his rights.

"Do you have proof? Where's the proof?" asked Kevin when the officer finished.

The Johnsons were now surprised.

"We'll give you the proof when we get to the police station," said Officer Rodriguez as she put Kevin into the backseat of the police car.

Question: How did Officer Rodriguez know Kevin was the shooter?

<u>Answer</u>: Officer Reeves stood to Peter's left, and Peter was shot in the right arm. The bullet removed from Peter's arm was from a revolver. Officer Reeves had never owned or purchased a revolver. Jill was Kevin's niece, and Kevin didn't like Peter peeking through Jill's bedroom window.

Who's The Flag Thief?

It was the Friday before Memorial Day and volunteers decided to put small flags on the graves of the deceased military personnel in the local cemetery. Near the cemetery, there was a dam and a family of beavers also lived nearby.

Joe Stephens, the head volunteer, had everyone come out early Friday morning.

"I want to thank you all for coming out so early on Friday morning to put flags on all the graves of our deceased military service men and women," Joe said. "I deeply appreciate it."

"My wife, Gertrude, and I are both retired from the United States Air Force," John Stoner said. "We mainly sit at home and do nothing, so we're glad to be here today."

"Besides, our six children are all in the military, so we're empty nesters," Gertrude added.

"Let's all get to work," Joe said.

All the volunteers began putting flags on graves throughout the cemetery. They were finished two hours later. Afterwards, all the volunteers hugged each other and went home.

Early Saturday morning, Floyd Mattingly, the groundskeeper, arrived and discovered that all the flags were gone. He made a phone call to his brother, Officer Jack Mattingly. Officer Jack came out immediately to take a report.

"Yesterday, a group of volunteers came and put flags on all the graves of our deceased military people. Today, all the flags are gone," Floyd told Officer Jack.

"Who would take small flags on wooden sticks?" asked Jack as he opened his pad. "They're not items of high value. Nobody can pawn them for money."

"I'm just as confused as you are," responded Floyd.

"Do you have surveillance cameras around here?"

"The camera repair people are coming in today to fix them. Also, the cameras are connected to my phone. After the cameras start working again, we'll find out who the flag thief is."

"Get the cameras fixed," said Officer Jack as he closed his pad.

Floyd posted about the flag theft incident on social media. That afternoon, some local high school students came with small flags to place on the graves of the military service people. All the high school students were finished within an hour.

Shannon Choi, a local news reporter, came to the cemetery to cover the story.

"Yesterday, a group of volunteers who are retired from various branches of the military put small flags onto the graves of our deceased local military service people. All the flags were stolen, and the cameras were not working at the time," Shannon reported. "This morning, a group of local high school students came out to put more flags on the graves."

Shannon pointed to the local high school students and some of them waved into the camera.

Floyd stepped in front of the camera. "I plan to press charges against those who are responsible. Theft is theft! They were small flags on wooden sticks and they're of no financial value. They cannot be pawned for money, so none of this makes any sense."

Early Sunday morning, Floyd arrived at the cemetery. All the flags had disappeared again. Floyd made another phone call to Officer Jack. Again, Officer Jack arrived immediately.

"Jack, they did it again. But this time, the cameras are working." Floyd fiddled with his smartphone. "We'll soon find out who the flag thief is."

Officer Jack pulled out his pad as he viewed the video on Floyd's phone. Floyd and Jack both burst out laughing at the same time.

"I guess I'm not going to press charges." Floyd chuckled.

Floyd posted the video of the flag thief on social media. Everyone who watched the video of the local flag thief also started laughing.

Sunday afternoon, the first group of volunteers came out after church to put more flags on the graves. They all laughed as they placed the flags on the graves.

"What's so funny about someone stealing flags?" John fussed.

Floyd pulled out his phone and showed John the video of the flag thief.

John also laughed.

Question: Who was the flag thief?

<u>Answer</u>: The alleged flag thief was a beaver. She needed the wooden sticks to help build her "house" on the dam.

Why Does Fred Need the Wheelchair?

Fred Sweet walked around Japer Street. Robert Sanderson sat in his wheelchair in his front yard.

Fred approached Robert. "How are you doing today?" he asked.

"I'm doing well," Robert answered. "I'm sitting out here watching all our neighbors doing their yardwork. How are you doing?"

"Did you hear about my car accident last month? A bus from a private school hit the back of my car and I injured my neck."

"You already told me that story, and you said you injured your back."

"It was my neck and my back. I received a fifty-thousand dollar settlement."

"Good for you. How much money did you get in your other lawsuit last summer?"

"I sued the Meadows family for twenty-five-thousand since they had a faulty lounge chair and I injured myself after the legs on one side fell off."

"From what I hear, you invited yourself to their reunion."

"The Meadows family is prosperous. Some of them are over-the-road truck drivers. Some are CDL Parcel Delivery drivers. Others are nurses or pharmacists. They have plenty of money. I should have sued them for two-hundred-fifty-thousand."

"That family is prosperous, but not that prosperous. Because of you, the judge told them they cannot have a family reunion for five years."

"I also got lawsuit money from a slip and fall at the appliance assembly job six months ago. My fall was in the men's bathroom. I got twenty-thousand from that."

"Of course, the bathrooms are the only places without cameras."

"How have you been feeling?"

"My cancer returned, and the doctors are giving me less than a year to live."

Fred leaned closer to Robert. "When you die, can I get your wheelchair?" Fred whispered.

"No! You cannot have my wheelchair. I plan to donate my wheelchair back to the military veterans' hospital."

"Why would you do a stupid thing like that?"

"The army gave me this wheelchair after an enemy sniper shot me during Desert Storm. When I die, they get it back. Why do you need my wheelchair, anyway?" Robert was furious.

"You need to stop being so selfish!"

"Ophelia Wilson allowed you to borrow her late husband's wheelchair after one of your so-called accidents, and you charged her a thousand dollars to get it back!"

"Mr. Wilson left her with plenty of money. She was able to afford to pay me."

"What you need to do is get a job and stop suing everyone!"

All the other neighbors on Japer Street stopped what they were doing and walked towards Robert's house. They then began to whisper among each other.

"Please keep your voice down. People are looking at us." Fred was embarrassed.

"I don't care! Why do you want my wheelchair?! You walk around just fine! I wish I could still walk around Japer Street. I joined the army after high school. Enemy snipers in the Middle East shot me in the back, and the bullet paralyzed me from the waist down! That's why I'm in a wheelchair!" Robert was outraged.

The onlookers looked at Fred and waited for an answer.

"This doesn't involve any of you!" Fred shouted. "This conversation is only between Robert and me! All of you are being nosy!"

"All the nosy neighbors on Japer Street want to hear an answer from Frederick Sweet!" chanted Robert.

"I might need it, just in case something happens to me again."

"No!" shouted Robert. "You will not get my wheelchair! After I die, the military veterans' hospital will get the wheelchair back. Again, why do you *allegedly* need my wheelchair?"

Looking around, Fred was afraid to answer the question.

<u>Question</u>: Why did Fred "allegedly" need Robert's wheelchair?"

<u>Answer</u>: Fred was a "career" scammer who always found ways to sue people and companies. He planned to either "stage" more accidents or deliberately allow himself to get injured so he could sue companies or insurance agencies. The wheelchair would become part of his "scam". The military veterans' hospital got the wheelchair back after Robert died.

Why Was Barney the Burglary Victim?

Barney Lile approached his cousin, Andrew Taylor.

"Our grandparents left us each two-million dollars!" Barney shouted.

"Not too loud," whispered Andrew. "We don't want the whole town to know."

"I'm going to continue to keep my custodial job at Kentville High School. Do you plan to keep yours as a professor at Kentville Community College?"

"Of course, I plan to keep my job," responded Andrew.

"You don't want to retire and enjoy the money?"

"No. I want to be an example for my son, Ron. Since I'm a widower, Aunt Brenda will have guardianship over the money until Ron becomes eighteen if I die anytime soon."

"I plan to put my two million into a savings account and live off the interest. I'm finally going to propose marriage to Louise. We'll then live off my janitorial salary, her waitress salary, and the monthly interest."

"I also plan to put my two-million dollars into a savings account and live off the monthly interest. Aunt Brenda is retired from the Kentville School System, and she draws a monthly retirement check. We plan to live off my college professor money, her retirement money, and the interest. None of us are to broadcast anything about the inheritance money. Agreed?"

"Agreed." Barney was hesitant.

Andrew and Barney deposited their checks into Kentville Bank and Trust.

"Since it's summer vacation, I'm going to spend the summer buying new things."

"Just be careful," warned Andrew.

Andrew kept his finances a secret from others in town. Barney blabbed about his finances as well as about all the items he bought.

On Monday, Barney had an industrial-sized washer and dryer delivered to his house. On Tuesday, he bought a new bedroom set. On Wednesday, he bought other new furniture. On Thursday, he bought a new wardrobe. Friday morning, he bought a seventy-two-inch widescreen TV.

Oscar Greenwood and Grover Blue were the two garbage collectors. Grover drove the garbage truck, and Oscar collected the garbage. Fridays were garbage pickup days in Kentville.

"Wow!" shouted Oscar when he saw all the boxes on the curb. "Barney must have lots of new and fancy items in his house!"

"That's what it looks like," Grover said as he got out of the truck to help Oscar with all the boxes. "He should cut up all these boxes and put them into black garbage bags."

"You're right," Oscar agreed. "That's what Andrew does."

Barney stepped outside. "I guess you two are jealous. Ever since I received my inheritance money, I've been shopping online. It's nice to be rich."

After Grover and Oscar were finished, they went off to the next house.

Barney and Louise got married the following Saturday. They spent their one-month honeymoon in San Juan, Puerto Rico.

They returned from their trip to a ransacked and burglarized house. Louise called the police immediately.

Officers James Reeves and Victor Rodriguez arrived and took the report.

"I congratulated your cousin, Andrew. He married Helen last Saturday, and they're spending a month-long honeymoon in San Juan," Victor commented.

"Before going on their honeymoon, Andrew invested in an up-to-date security system," James said. "You might want to do the same for your house."

"Nothing like this ever happened to Andrew," whined Barney. "He has an eighty-four-inch widescreen TV. Nobody ever burglarized him. Why did this happen to us?"

"Will the insurance cover everything?" Victor asked.

"I hope so. I guess Louise and I will spend a week at Andrew's house while you two do your investigation."

"We'll find out who did this," James assured them.

Barney and Louise spent the week at Andrew's house.

Later in the week, Louise got off her mobile phone. "I just got off the phone, and the homeowners' insurance can only replace our items one time," Louise said. "If this continues to happen, then they cannot help us."

"That's what I was afraid of," Barney replied.

<u>Question</u>: Why was Barney burglarized, and who robbed him?

<u>Answer</u>: Barney blabbed to others about all his possessions. He even put empty boxes outside for others to see. Oscar and Grover were the burglars. Both will spend time in jail.

Word Salad

Salina Vila was a Psychology Professor at Kentville University. She took her students on a field trip to the Kentville Mental hospital. Mr. Roy Burris, the school dean, also came along. They were visiting Salina's fraternal twin sister, Kalina. Excited, Kalina ran out of the front door and into the visiting area, wearing overalls over her hospital gown.

"Yoo-yoos! Yee-yees! Yoo-yoos! Yee-yees! Yoo-yoos! Yee-yees! Yoo-yoos! Yee-yees!" Kalina excitedly shouted as she ran toward the crowd of students.

John French was half-black and half-white, and he had short, curly hair. Floyd Tatum was an African-American man with a short afro.

"You have yoo-yoos," Kalina said as she pointed to John's curly hair.

"You have a yee-yee," she said as she pointed to Floyd's afro.

Kalina pointed to the overalls of Jim Brown, an older student.

"You wear odos," Salina said as she pointed to Jim's overalls. "I wear odos too." She pointed to her own overalls.

A security guard on a horse rode through the visiting area.

"A hee-hee!" shouted Kalina as she pointed to the horse and ran to pet it.

"I brought you students here so you can meet my fraternal twin sister, Kalina Meadows. She's been like this since we were small children," Salina told her students.

John raised his hand and Salina pointed to him.

"Can I ask how she became like this?" he asked.

"That's an excellent question," Salina said. "It's said that in the womb, twins 'fight' to be the first one born. I was born first, and she was born second. She was born feet first and fighting for oxygen. Being without oxygen for a long period of time had an impact on her mental development. Physically, we're just alike, but mentally, we're not."

Floyd raised his hand and Salina pointed to him.

"If you ever get married and have children, could they have the same kind of mental challenges, or differences, as Kalina?" asked Floyd.

"Her mental state isn't genetic," Salina explained. "To be honest, there were men who never married me because they were afraid of our having children with the same mental differences as Kalina. When I married Luis Vila, he didn't feel like that."

Jim removed his baseball cap and hung his head in sadness.

"When I was five-months pregnant, Luis was shot and killed while working at the auto shop that Jim and he worked at together." Salina grew sad. "I was so traumatized that I had a miscarriage. During my miscarriage, I started bleeding, and the doctors had to perform a hysterectomy to stop the bleeding. I buried my husband and our unborn daughter next to each other. I named our daughter Luisa Kalina Vila. I cannot become pregnant ever again."

"Why did you put Kalina here?" John asked.

"Kentville Mental Hospital has a fully trained staff and the facility is designed for those with mental challenges like Kalina. I cannot care for her like they can," Salina answered.

"All of you need to imagine yourselves in Salina's situation," Dean Burris suggested.

"None of us are judging," Floyd said.

"Salina's insight into various kinds of mental challenges is the reason why she's the best Psychology Professor in Kentville's history," Dean Burris continued.

All the students clapped for Salina.

Salina and Kalina hugged each other. The staff then had Kalina go back inside.

Salina and her class all got back onto the bus. Dean Burris was the bus driver.

Jim raised his hand and Salina pointed to him.

"I'm aware that "odos" are overalls and a "hee-hee" is a horse. But I'm curious about what "yoo-yoos" and a "yee-yee" are."

"She pointed to my hair and said that I have yoo-yoos," John said.

"She then pointed to my hair and said that I have a yee-yee," Floyd added.

"It has to do with hair texture." Salina laughed and then explained what Kalina meant by the terms "yoo-yoos" and "yee-yee".

Question: What are "yoo-yoos" and a "yee-yee"?

Answer: To Kalina, "yoo-yoos" are short curls, and a "yee-yee" is an afro. Some people with various kinds of mental challenges (or differences) have their own invented words. This term is called a "Word Salad".

Zombie Apocalypse in Louisville!

It was the end of summer. Coy and Cami Gordon decided to visit Louisville, Kentucky. It was Friday night, and they went to the popular nightlife attractions on Baxter Avenue. As they walked into a pizza joint, they saw zombies walking towards them! What was going on?

There were hundreds of zombies walking down Baxter Avenue. Men zombies, women zombies, and children as zombies. There were even baby zombies in strollers! Some zombies were even dogs. As Coy and Cami walked into the pizza place, all the customers were watching with amusement. What's so amusing about a zombie apocalypse? Even the servers watched with excitement. Normal people would be screaming and running away! Is it the end of the world? What's going on? Zombies even peeked into the windows of the pizza joint!

Coy ordered the thin-crust pepperoni and cheese lovers pizza. They both ordered soft drinks. As Coy and Cami dined, they became less afraid of the zombies. Nobody around them seemed frightened.

"Zombies have been invading Baxter Avenue annually for many years," the server said as he gave Coy the ticket.

Coy and Cami paid the bill, left a tip and exited the restaurant. They walked down the street to their friends' house. Their friends, Bobby Ray and LeeAnn McCoy, both watched the zombies from their living room window with amazement. The McCoys' three children, Joseph, Jesse, and Jazmine also watched the zombies, from their bedroom windows. Coy and Cami were in the guest bedroom, unable to sleep. Cami looked out the window and still saw zombies walking down the sidewalk. Some zombies even looked up at her.

Saturday afternoon, Coy and Cami went to *Fourth Street Live!* and there were more karaoke bars and nightclubs than they could choose from. They chose to go into the first nightclub they saw. They ordered the twenty-dollar limitless chicken wings with limitless soft drinks. As they were enjoying their lunch, they saw zombies walking down *Fourth Street Live!*

"Again?" Cami shouted. "They seem to be everywhere! What's going on?"

After Coy paid for the meals and left a tip, they walked out of the nightclub. Terrified, Coy and Cami both walked back to the McCoys' house. The McCoys were watching the local news.

"Zombies are taking over Baxter Avenue and Fourth Street Live!" Shannon Choi, the local news reporter, said. "Louisville, Kentucky is now facing a Zombie Apocalypse!"

The McCoys laughed at the horrified looks on Coy and Cami's faces.

Later that evening, the McCoy family walked out of their bedrooms. They had suddenly become a family of zombies! They walked out the door and down the sidewalk, to join all the other zombies. Coy and Cami packed their luggage and got into their car. They drove all the way back to Cincinnati, Ohio that night.

"Did you enjoy your visit to Louisville?" Dale Gordon, Coy's father, asked.

"We want to hear all about it," Dawn Gordon, Coy's mother, said.

"You won't believe us!" Cami responded.

"Of course, we will." Dawn laughed.

"We drove all the way home," Coy said. "We're ready for bed now."

"We'll tell you two all about it in the morning," Cami said as she and Coy carried their luggage into their bedroom.

The next morning, Dale and Dawn fixed breakfast for Coy and Cami.

"You two will not believe this," Cami said between bites of bacon. "There were zombies all over downtown Louisville and Baxter Avenue."

"What was so strange, nobody was afraid of them," Coy said.

"Spectators were amused and entertained by the Zombie Apocalypse," Cami said.

"There's no reason to be afraid." Dawn laughed. "Louisville has a Zombie Apocalypse every year during the summertime."

"The Zombie Apocalypse is not what you see on TV." Dale laughed. "In fact, it's fun to watch. There's no reason to be afraid."

Answer: Louisville, Kentucky had a "Zombie Festival" every year in August. There were no Zombie Festivals in 2020 and 2021. After the pandemic, the Zombie Festival was restarted in 2022. Now, *The Louisville Annual Zombie Festival* can occur during various times of the year.

Other Books by this Author

Purchase at www.roystonchildrenbookstore.com

I Have A lot To SAY

D. E. MADDOX

Purchase at: https://www.amazon.com/Have-ALot-Dorothea-Elizabeth-Maddox/dp/1955063079/